THE
MYSTERY MAN

BOOKS BY SCOTT CORBETT

THE
MYSTERY MAN

by Scott Corbett

Illustrated by
Nathan Goldstein

An Atlantic Monthly Press Book
Little, Brown and Company
Boston   Toronto

LIBRARY OF CONGRESS CATALOG CARD NO. 70-108170

Second Printing

ATLANTIC—LITTLE, BROWN BOOKS
ARE PUBLISHED BY
LITTLE, BROWN AND COMPANY
IN ASSOCIATION WITH
THE ATLANTIC MONTHLY PRESS

Published simultaneously in Canada
by Little, Brown & Company (Canada) Limited

PRINTED IN THE UNITED STATES OF AMERICA

To
WILLIAM PAXTON,
who knows Silas well

1694799

THE
MYSTERY MAN

1

Normally Tod Emmet slept like any other boy his age. Normally the roof could have fallen in and not waked him, once he was asleep. But just now, as his right side reminded him, he was not exactly normal. Every so often he got into a position that hurt and made him wake up. That was what had happened to him now. The thunder had nothing to do with it.

He listened to the sound die away like a distant drum roll, ominous and foreboding in the blackness of the night. Groaning in much the same low key, he shifted onto his back and gingerly touched the place, still tender, where doctors had sewed him up after his operation.

Depression settled over him like that raven in the poem by Edgar Allan Poe they had studied in Mr. Caxton's English class. Thinking of Mr. Caxton made him think of vocabulary-building — old Wild Bill was

3

always hammering away at vocabulary-building — and that led him to think about two unpleasant words he had recently added to his vocabulary the hard way. Vermiform appendix.

Why did people have to have such things? His vermiform appendix had brought him acute appendicitis, with some bad complications that had made it a serious matter. He had been rushed to the hospital and operated on, and now he was missing the last month of school.

Not that he couldn't bear up under that blow. Nor was he unhappy about being away from home for a week, because he was in one of his favorite places, his Uncle Gary's small resort inn near the seashore. Even his mother had been forced to admit it was the perfect place for him to recuperate. At first she had planned to give up going with his father to a business convention in San Francisco. But then Uncle Gary had offered to take care of Tod while they were gone, and she had agreed.

A chance to get to the shore a whole two weeks before the end of school! That part had sounded good enough to make even appendicitis worthwhile. But of course the very thing that made it possible for him to be there made it impossible for him to take full advantage of the situation. He couldn't race to the beach and go swimming. He couldn't prowl around in the woods that surrounded the inn. He couldn't even play catch with his Uncle Gary. He had to sit around recuperating!

Punching his pillow, Tod squirmed his way carefully into a more comfortable position. The house was so still he could hear the grandfather's clock downstairs in the front parlor measuring time with its slow, deliberate, melancholy ticks. He listened, and his mind went straying off into night thoughts. It was almost creepy to think about all the empty rooms around him. He was alone in his wing of the inn. His uncle was the only other person in the whole house, at the other end of a long hall. Tod wondered how many other people had ever waked up right where he was, in the middle of this big bed in the middle of the night in this old, old house. George Washington might have slept here if he had ever come to Bell Harbor. People had slept in this room when Massachusetts was still a British colony.

A dim flash of sheet lightning outlined his bedroom windows, and then they blacked out again, and another mutter of distant thunder came rolling along like a ponderous warning. The air was thick and heavy. It would be raining buckets any minute now. He decided he had better get up and close the windows. Uncle Gary was having enough trouble with leaks the roof had developed, without having to mop up puddles under windows.

From his room Tod could see the driveway circle at the side of the house, and part of the back lawn in the direction of the guest cottages that fronted on it. He had padded across the room to the windows and was reaching up with his left hand to close one — he had to be careful about stretching, especially his right side — when a sound out in the dark made him stop.

It was a soft, grating sound. Leaning on the window-sill, he peered into blackness, hoping to get a glimpse of some animal. That old raccoon, maybe, who kept figuring out ways to get into the garbage cans faster than Uncle Gary thought of ways to keep him out.

Again Tod heard the sound. This time the grating was sharper, and had a muffled ring to it. Like metal on stone. He waited, listening hard, but heard nothing more.

Then something moved on the back lawn. A gray-black shadow, gray-black against black, a fuzz of movement in the dark. A blur, but large, and upright.

A man!

Tod's heart bumped. Who was prowling around out there? He hesitated. Should he shout at the prowler and scare him off, or slip down the hall to his uncle's room and tell him someone was —

Before he could decide, a flash of lightning turned the night ghastly white and transformed the shadow into a tall, lean old man carrying a long-handled spade. A crash of thunder made Tod jump as blackness blotted out the livid lightning flash and the figure disappeared.

If the ghost of some colonial gravedigger had flick-ered across the lawn, it could not have been more

spectral. Yet Tod was more startled than scared — because he knew who it was.

"For Pete's sake!" said Tod to himself. "What's *he* up to?"

The man was M. M. Murkey — the Mystery Man, as he still called himself. What was old M.M. doing outside in the middle of the night with a spade? Was that what had made the sounds Tod heard?

M.M. had been walking toward the corner of the house when Tod caught his glimpse of him. A moment later Tod sensed more than saw a dim form returning. The glare of another lightning flash showed him that the old man was crossing the back lawn on his way to the guest cottage he occupied, hurrying now as the first patter of large raindrops began to fall.

Again Tod hesitated. Why wake up his uncle now? He could tell him about what he had seen in the morning. But what had old M.M. been up to? When he had reappeared just now, he was no longer carrying the spade. What had he used it for?

Lightning flashed and thunder crashed almost at the same instant, and rain pounded down as though a million fighter planes were suddenly strafing the inn with liquid bullets. Tod was again reaching up to close the windows when the sound of his door being opened stealthily made him whirl.

A round-faced man peered in at him through round glasses.

8

"Tod!"

"Uncle Gary! Gosh, you scared me!"

"Well, that makes us even!"

One of Uncle Gary's guests had once described him as "well-rounded — and I don't mean he's read a lot!" Though he was not fat, everything about him fitted the description, from his generous paunch to his bald head, which was as round as a honeydew melon and had the same waxy pallor.

"I didn't expect to find you awake," he said. "I wanted to check your windows. Here, don't strain yourself, I'll close them."

"My side woke me up. But listen, guess what I saw?"

"What?"

Tod told him. Uncle Gary listened, and shook his bald head in a resigned way.

"What now? I tell you, that old coot gets nuttier every year — and he's been coming here for twenty! A spade, eh? What could he have been doing?"

"Whatever it was, he sure wanted to keep it a secret!"

"Hmm!" said Uncle Gary, and it was all Tod could do to keep from laughing. He knew his uncle very well, and he knew that nobody had a more well-rounded bump of curiosity. If there was one thing Uncle Gary couldn't stand, it was a secret. Show him a secret, and he couldn't wait to ferret out the inside story. He was a born gossip, and since he was also an innkeeper, the only thing that saved him from ruin was that he was never malicious or mean.

"Well," he said now, "last night M.M. asked me to drive him over to the bus station in the morning. Said he had to go up to Boston to tend to some business. After he goes we'll have a look around and see if we can find where he was doing his midnight gardening."

He shook his head again.

"The Mystery Man! It's a long, long time since he ran that Mystery Man program of his on radio, but he's never gotten over it. I've never seen anyone who loves mysterious goings-on more than he does. You watch, tomorrow. He'll throw out hints about something or other, and chuckle his famous Mystery Man chuckle that millions out there in radio land used to know so well!"

"That chuckle!" said Tod. "He must be eighty years old, and he acts sillier than most kids I know!"

Tod's scorn was so lofty, so intolerant, so pompous that it brought a tolerant twinkle to his uncle's bright eyes.

"Tod, your trouble is that you expect grown-ups to grow up. Well, they never do, really. Some do more than others, but nobody does in all ways. If you start going through life expecting grown-ups to really act like grown-ups all the time, you're going to be disappointed. Lots of people don't really grow up at all, they just grow older. And it works both ways. Children spend a lot of time acting grown-up, and grown-ups spend a lot of time acting childish." He chuckled as he added, "Why, if I expected all my guests to act like grown-ups, I'd be driven out of my mind in a month! No, you have to take them as they are."

Tod knew his uncle's philosophy helped to explain why he was a good innkeeper, if not a rich one. But still, an old geezer like M.M.! . . . Maybe in his case it was second childhood. Tod changed the subject by asking a question that had been on his mind ever since the old man had arrived two days ago.

"If he was such a big hit on radio, why didn't he do his show on television?"

"He hated TV. Said it spoiled the illusion. Anyway, by the time television really took over, he was already pretty old, and he'd made a fortune, so he retired. It was after that when he started coming down here for a couple of weeks every spring — always before the season started, to take advantage of out-of-season rates. It's no wonder he has a lot of money. He knows how to hang onto it!"

Lightning flashed, thunder rumbled, and rain rattled hard on the windows.

"Look at it come down!" said Tod. His uncle looked, and groaned.

"Just what I don't need! I guess I'd better check around and see if my patchwork on the roof did the job."

Tod trailed along. There was no sign of leaks — yet, at least — in any of the upstairs rooms.

"Maybe I really caught them this time," said Uncle Gary, pathetically hopeful. "The kitchen should tell the tale."

The kitchen had a tale to tell, all right. They found Pearl, Uncle Gary's old golden retriever, looking resentfully at a wet place on the floor alongside the stove.

"Right where she likes to sleep!" said Tod. "Wouldn't you know it?"

"Fast as I patch one spot, another springs a leak!"

Uncle Gary swore under his breath as he set a pan in place to catch the slow drips. He glowered up at the ceiling.

"I guess there's no answer but a new roof. But what a time of year to have to lay out that much money!"

The local roofing expert had given him an estimate of the cost, and Tod knew it came to two thousand dollars. Anyone within half a mile would have known it when Uncle Gary first heard the sum and repeated it.

Tod went to the door and looked out. With the kitchen light on, he could see the tool shed. Leaning against the shed he could see a long-handled spade, its steel surface gleaming blackly in the rain.

"There's the spade," said Tod. "He was in such a hurry he didn't put it away."

His uncle took a look.

"No, I'm the guilty party. He didn't leave it there, I did. That's where I left it yesterday."

"Oh! Then he put it back exactly where he found it, so nobody would know he used it."

"Be just like him," admitted Uncle Gary. "M. M. Murkey, the Mystery Man. Lord only knows what he's up to now — but maybe tomorrow we can fool him and find out!"

2

The next time Tod woke up, sunshine was streaming in through the windows. It was one of those especially beautiful mornings, as though the weather were apologizing for its bad behavior the night before — the sort of morning when the only sensible thing to do was race to the beach. But instead . . .

He turned gloomy eyes toward a quartet of paperback books that were elbowing each other between two book-ends atop the chest of drawers. He gazed at them, and remembered the reaction of his English teacher to his predicament.

"Well, one nice thing, Tod," Mr. Caxton had said, with a wicked twinkle in his eye, "this will give you a chance to get a head start on your summer reading list!"

Silas Marner. The Master of Ballantrae. A Tale of Two Cities. Ivanhoe. Each book got bigger, and he intended to read them in that order, the smallest one first.

Besides reading the four books, he was supposed to study his English, math, science, and history to keep up with his class. A cheerful prospect.

He dressed as quickly as he could — it was a nuisance, having to move carefully — and started to hurry downstairs. He was eager to find out if M.M. had shown up for breakfast yet.

From the kitchen came a shout.

"Walk!"

"I am!" called Tod, and did his best to slow down to an invalid's gait. But it was a bore.

The Old Manse, as Uncle Gary's inn was called, was a rambling colonial house with low ceilings, wide-board floors, and windows with lots of small panes in them. The oldest part of the house had been built two hundred and fifty years ago by the local minister, which explained its name.

Later on other sections had been tacked onto the original house, in typical New England style, until now there were eight rooms upstairs and a couple of large bedrooms downstairs, along with a sitting room, a front parlor, a dining room, the kitchen, and a laundry room. Uncle Gary ran everything very informally, so that it was an easy place to feel at home in, especially for Tod.

"Bring me the bus schedule, will you?" his uncle

called as Tod reached the foot of the stairs. "I think I left it in the mail drawer."

"Okay!"

Tod detoured to the front parlor, where an old-fashioned stand-up writing desk near the south windows served as the inn's registration desk and mail repository. Like so many things in the Old Manse, the writing desk was an authentic part of the house. The grandfather's clock had been given to the minister by his father. The spinning wheel that sat beside the original fireplace had belonged to the minister's wife. The flintlock fowling piece that hung over the mantel had been the minister's own gun with which he had often provided something extra for the table. The sextant in the glass case on a side table had been used in all corners of the seven seas by a grandson who became a shipmaster. As for the writing desk, Uncle Gary had found it in the attic, with the name of still another descendant carefully carved into the face of its drawer.

Since the new season had not quite started, Uncle Gary had not as yet set the inn's guest register out on the desk. It was just as well, too, because the desk's slightly slanted top was gleaming wet. Tod stared up at the ceiling.

"Oh, boy!"

It was water-stained, straight above the desk.

During the season, guests' mail was kept in the deep

drawer under the desk top. It was slightly ajar. Tod pulled it open and took out the two soggy items it contained.

One was a bus schedule. The other was a manila envelope addressed to A. G. Cartwright and marked "Book."

Tod turned to rush news of this latest catastrophe to headquarters.

"Uncle Gary! We've got a bad —"

"Walk!"

"But Uncle Gary —"

"What's the matter?"

His uncle looked around from the stove, where he was breaking eggs into a skillet for Tod's breakfast.

"There's a leak in the front parlor, and the mail drawer got soaked!"

Uncle Gary stared at him blankly. Then the message registered. He grabbed some towels and set out for the disaster area. Tod tossed the wet mail and the bus schedule on a kitchen table and followed.

"This is the sort of thing that would turn my hair gray if I had any," said Uncle Gary as he mopped out the mail drawer and dried off the desk top. "Everything upstairs was all right, so I never thought to take a look in here. But I can see what happened. There's a place alongside the chimney — I thought I'd fixed it, but — Well, this settles it. I might as well face it. I've got to have a new roof put on."

Poor Uncle Gary looked so worried that Tod began to think some bitter thoughts about rain and leaky roofs and roofers who charged a fortune to put on new ones. It seemed wrong that anyone as good-hearted as Uncle Gary should have to worry about such things. But then, of course, that was Uncle Gary's trouble, according to his brother George, Tod's father — "Gary's too darn generous for his own good. He'll never make any money with that inn of his. He's such a good host, he'll bankrupt himself!"

Well, that was what Uncle Gary enjoyed being. He wasn't going to change, and at least he got a lot of fun out of life when he wasn't *too* pressed for money. In fact, sometimes Tod could not escape the painful thought that his uncle got more fun out of life than his father did, for all his success in business. Sometimes he wished his father . . . But then, right now, here was poor Uncle Gary in a bind, fighting the endless battle of keeping an old house in repair.

"Hey, I left your eggs on the fire!" he remembered, and hurried back to rescue them. Following him, Tod watched the round man bustle across the dining room and found himself grinning, because there was something lovably comic about his uncle's movements. Bustling was the only way to describe them. He never strolled anywhere slowly. He bustled. With his good-sized stomach leading the way, he looked (as Tod's father once remarked) like a busy workman pushing a wheelbarrow.

While Uncle Gary put the eggs on a plate and added a few strips of bacon, Tod examined A. G. Cartwright's soggy package. Its flap had come unglued.

"Who's A. G. Cartwright?"

"I don't know, but he's coming today," said Uncle Gary in an unhappy tone of voice. "That package came yesterday, and early this morning he called up to reserve a room. Worse yet, I told him he had some mail here, and he sounded as if that was important to him."

He eyed Mr. Cartwright's package gloomily.

"This will make a big hit with a new guest!"

Tod flipped the flap.

"Look, it's come open. There's a book in it. Looks like a paperback," he said, peering inside. "Maybe we can dry it out."

Automatically his uncle started to protest the idea of examining someone else's mail. But then he had second thoughts about it. Because if it was already open anyway, and if it was only a book, and not private correspondence . . .

"Well, what have we got to lose? Let's see it."

Tod pulled out the book. It wasn't too bad. Just bad enough so that you knew at once no amount of drying would ever make it look like new.

When he pulled it out, the book's back cover was showing. When he turned it over, Tod's face brightened.

"Hey, look! It's *Silas Marner!*"

Uncle Gary was not exactly thrilled by this news. "So?"

"So I've got a brand new copy of *Silas Marner*, and the same kind as this one! I recognize the cover!"

"Oh!"

Now his uncle began to show interest. Tod examined the manila envelope.

"Look — his name and address are typed, so they didn't smear. We could dry out the envelope, and put my copy in it, and . . ."

Behind the round glasses, Uncle Gary's eyes were flashing busily.

"Why, that would be tampering with the U.S. Mail!" he pointed out in a stern voice that failed to sound too convincing. "We could go to jail for doing such a thing. However . . . even the Supreme Court says it's the spirit of the law, not the letter of the law, that counts, and there's nothing wrong with our spirit. We have only the best interests of everybody at heart — especially mine. So we'll do it! Go get your copy, while I figure out how to dry this envelope. And walk!"

When Tod returned, Uncle Gary was out in the laundry room, off the kitchen, plugging in an electric iron.

"This ought to do it. Let's see your book. By George, you're right! Same cover, same edition. What a piece of luck! Shows we can't lose 'em all. I'll buy you a fresh copy if I can find one over in Hynesport when I take M.M. to the bus."

"Don't worry about it. I can probably read this one okay after it's dried out."

His uncle looked at him fondly and said, "You see, I knew what I was doing when I said for you to come down here, Tod. You always bring me luck," he declared, which of course made his favorite nephew feel very good. "Now go eat your eggs before they get cold."

While Tod was still eating at the kitchen table, Uncle Gary came back with the manila envelope neatly pressed and the book inside. He found some paste to seal the flap.

"How's that, Tod?"

"Great! Now I'll put it back in the mail drawer, and we're in business again."

"Right. And close the drawer tight!"

"Don't worry!"

Tod glanced out into the dining room.

"Has M.M. come over for breakfast yet?"

"Not yet. I guess prancing around in the middle of the night with that spade must have taken it out of him. I've never known him to sleep this late before. I hope he didn't overdo."

Uncle Gary sounded genuinely concerned. He had a capacity for caring about people, all kinds of people, even old windbags like M.M., that was amazing. Tod thought about it while he took A. G. Cartwright's package back to the mail drawer and stood the wet copy of *Silas Marner* in a sunny window with the pages fanned out to dry. It was really something, the way his uncle could be so nice to someone like that, an old man who expected a lot of extra attention and was quick to complain if the least little thing didn't suit him. It seemed to Tod that people like M.M. took advantage of his uncle's boundless good nature, and he resented it.

When he returned to the kitchen, he found Uncle Gary looking out the back windows.

"Here he comes!"

M.M. was all dressed up in his city clothes, right up to his gray fedora hat. He was wearing the vest of his dark blue suit, even though it was nearly summer. They watched the old man cross the lawn. He moved with something less than his usual spry step.

"He doesn't look up to snuff, Tod."

"I wonder what he'll have to say about last night?"

"Something mysterious — you'll see."

The back door scraped open, and M.M. appeared in the dining room. They both went out to say good morning.

"Better morning than night," the old man grumbled in his odd, hollow, booming voice. "That was a sock-dolager of a thunderstorm."

Uncle Gary fished for information.

"I hope it didn't get you up, or spoil your sleep."

Here it came, the special chuckle, right out of the radio land of olden times.

"Darn near spoiled more than that," said the Mystery Man cryptically, "but I managed."

Tod didn't dare look at his uncle. He would have grinned if he had. He had certainly never seen anyone like M. M. Murkey before. For one thing, the old boy was always putting on an act. He was like some hammy

23

old character actor who couldn't do anything naturally, who couldn't even pick up a magazine or put on his hat without making a production of it. He reminded Tod of Mr. Caxton when he started reading Shakespeare to them in class. But when he finished, Wild Bill didn't go right on being Shylock or King Richard, whereas M.M. never stopped being the Mystery Man.

A place was set at one of the tables for the inn's only guest. M.M.'s bones creaked as he folded his spare old frame down rather heavily into the chair, and Uncle Gary asked, "Your usual?"

"Is it ready?"

"Yes."

"Hmp. Can't waste it, then. But make it a small bowl."

"I'll bring it, Uncle Gary," Tod offered, and went out to the stove where he knew M.M.'s special breakfast food was simmering on a back burner. It was a thin gruel made of some special kind of health food cereal he insisted on having. Tod's opinion of it, when his uncle had given him a taste the previous morning, had been the same one he expressed now under his breath as he ladled a portion into a small bowl.

"Yuk!"

He put the bowl on a saucer and carried it in to the table. Yesterday morning M.M. had gobbled down a large bowl of the stuff with a greedy gusto that had amazed Tod. Today he showed no such enthusiasm. No

question about it, he was off his feed. It seemed to Tod that the gaunt old man's complexion was made up mostly of liver spots, and this morning there seemed to be more of them than ever, or perhaps they just stood out more against the unhealthy gray pallor of the rest of his face.

Uncle Gary brought M.M. tea and toast, and a cup of coffee for himself, and sat down to keep his guest company.

"That rain should have given the roof a pretty fair test," said M.M. "Any more leaks?"

"Worse than ever."

"Hmp. Well, don't look so down in the mouth." Again he treated them to the Mystery Man chuckle, and rolled his eyes sideways at Uncle Gary. "If things work out the way I want them to today, I'll *buy* you a new roof, and that's a promise!"

A new roof! Here was a thrilling promise indeed. Tod was surprised when his uncle failed to look excited. Instead Uncle Gary simply said, "Well, then, I hope things work out your way, M.M. That would be real nice."

"Well, why not? I've been coming here for a long time, and I'd like to do something extra for you, Gary. And as I say, if things work out right . . ."

His expression grew more mysterious than ever as his watery blue eyes narrowed and his chuckle deepened to a croak. He began to talk in riddles, as he loved to do.

Tod had only met the old man the day before — if you could call being nodded at and then ignored "meeting" him — but already he knew something about M.M.'s strange way of talking.

"That fool nephew of mine. Always looked down his nose at the Mystery Man — except for trying to get his hands on some of the money the Mystery Man made, him as never earned a nickel in his life. Neither nephew has, for that matter. Always enough trust fund income to scrape by on — bad thing! But Bertie's the one. Phinny is stupid and pretty well knows it, but Bertie has illusions. Thinks all the Mystery Man's codes and ciphers and clues were childish. Well, we'll see, we'll see," said M.M., and abruptly changed the subject. "What time does the next bus leave?"

Uncle Gary told him. M.M. consulted his big gold watch — the kind that hung on a chain in his vest pocket, and had a cover that snapped open when he wanted to look at the time.

"Then we'd better get cracking," he declared.

Uncle Gary eyed him with concern.

"M.M., you don't look well this morning. Why don't you take it easy today, and go up to Boston tomorrow?"

But the old man only showed annoyance, and became mysterious again.

"Nonsense, I'm fine. A little off the mark, maybe, but nothing serious. And I don't want to be around for a while. Said I wouldn't. Clear field for the idiot to make a fool of himself. Right under his nose. Any schoolboy could —" he began, and then stopped short, obviously struck by the fact that he had a schoolboy under his own nose. His glance swooped down. "Yes, sir, any schoolboy could figure it out."

With a sweep of his arm that was straight out of melodrama, he pointed a skeletal finger at Tod.

"Don't you help him now, boy!" he ordered, with a flash of humor. Tod was too surprised to reply, and the next instant M.M. had turned back to Uncle Gary.

"I know there's a four o'clock bus back, and I'll be on it. Meet me at five-thirty. Then we'll have some fun! Oh, yes, we'll have some fun!"

And this time his chuckle was a real masterpiece. For that matter, Tod had to give him credit for one thing: he did know how to create a mystery. What "fun" were they going to have when he came back that evening? Who was he planning to have fun with? What did it all have to do with his being out in the middle of the night with a spade? What was going on?

Whatever it was, Tod hoped his uncle would get a new roof out of it!

3

As soon as the men had left to drive to the bus station in Hynesport, Tod walked over to M.M.'s cottage. Circling it slowly, he examined the ground, looking for signs of recent digging.

The heavy rain had been no help. It would make fresh digging harder to detect. But even so a little close scrutiny should do the trick.

He could not find anything that looked like new spade marks anywhere around the cottage. If M.M. hadn't been digging here, where had he been?

There were four guest cottages. Two were at the end and two along the far side of the large rectangular back lawn. The lawn was bounded by bushes and underbrush, except on the side nearest the house. Behind the bushes the woods began. An awful lot of territory to cover; Tod scarcely knew where to start. M.M. had been out here somewhere digging. Tod had heard the

scrape of the spade on stones and pebbles. But where?

On second thought, he decided to wait till his uncle returned before looking around any more. Maybe Uncle Gary would have some ideas. Maybe M.M. would say something during their ride over to the bus station that would give them something to go on.

From the far edge of the lawn, the land fell away down a steep hillside. From there Tod could see the village with the white church steeple as its most prominent landmark. Second most prominent was the big old captain's house, with a widow's walk on its roof, that now housed Bell Harbor's public library.

Beyond the village he could see the dunes dotted with beach cottages, and beyond them the beach and the sea. Blue water sparkled and danced under a blue sky, throwing up small whitecaps into a stiff breeze, and washing up onto sandbars that were beginning to show as the tide ebbed. He tortured himself with this view for a few moments, wishing he could be fooling around out on the flats, investigating tidal pools, looking for horseshoe crabs and razor clams and sea worms and all the other interesting inhabitants of sand and shallows. It was terrible to be so near, and to think of all the fun he might have been having, and then to turn away and wonder how he was going to pass the time.

Wandering at loose ends, he went inside again and decided to check the front parlor to make sure the leak over the writing stand had completely dried up.

It seemed to have done so. As for the damaged book, its pages were dry now, but no amount of pressing would have made them look the same again. They were obviously water-stained, and so was the cover. Lucky thing he'd had that extra copy!

Still, the book was readable enough. He flipped through the pages, and was pleased to find there were only one hundred and eighty-five of them. That *Ivanhoe* probably had twice as many. Good old Silas. He weighed the small book in his hand. Well, why not? Why not get started? Think how virtuous he would look when Uncle Gary came back and found he'd started on his summer reading!

Book in hand, he went out to the sunny little patio in the angle of the house formed by the dining room and the kitchen, which extended several feet farther back than the dining room. On its other two sides the patio was bounded by the driveway circle and the back lawn. Here Uncle Gary always set up a couple of iron tables with umbrellas and a dozen canvas chairs for guests during the season. Leaving the book on the grass, he walked around to the tool shed to get out one of the folding chairs that were stored in it. There he stopped to look at the long-handled spade, still leaning against the shed where M.M. had left it.

Flinging his arm out like a junior Mystery Man, he said, "Speak, O Spade! Reveal to me what thou hast been delving into of late!"

The spade remained silent, so he switched to a tougher treatment. Grabbing it by its handle, he gave it a good shaking up.

"Okay, are you gonna talk, or do we hafta get rough?"

No answer. He leaned the spade against the shed again.

"All right for you, if that's your attitude. But I sure would like to hear what monkey business you've been up to!"

Tod took his chair to the patio, unfolded it, and settled himself to the task of beginning the story of *Silas Marner,* by George Eliot — George Eliot, who hadn't even been a man at all, but a woman whose real name was Mary Ann Evans. If that wasn't the final straw! But Mr. Caxton was determined to have the class read her silly old book, as he had been having his classes do for thirty years now, and that was that.

Tod opened the book to Part One, Chapter One, and began to read:

In the days when the spinning wheels hummed busily in the farmhouses — and even great ladies, clothed in silk and thread lace, had their toy spinning wheels of polished oak —

Spinning wheels. Tod paused and looked up at his uncle's inn. The story went back to those days. He thought about the spinning wheel that was sitting by the fireplace in the front parlor, and realized it must have hummed busily a couple of centuries ago, when the parson's wife used it to spin yarn to make her family's clothes with. Maybe he could stick some junk about that in his book report. Old Wild Bill would go for that (at school that was what they called Mr. William Caxton behind his back and in the annual school show: Wild Bill). Besides, some stuff about the inn and the spinning wheel would help pad out his report. Chuckling, Tod returned to his reading, starting over again:

In the days when the spinning wheels hummed busily in the farmhouses — and even great ladies, clothed in silk and thread lace, had their toy spinning wheels of polished oak — there might be seen, in districts far away among the lanes, or deep in the bosom of the hills, certain pallid undersized men who, by the side of the brawny countryfolk, looked like the remnants of a disinherited race. The shepherd's dog barked fiercely when one of

33

these alien-looking men appeared on the upland, dark against the early winter sunset; for what dog likes a figure bent under a heavy bag? — and these pale men rarely stirred abroad without that mysterious burden. . . .

Somewhere a dog had begun to bark. It was Pearl. Tod glanced up from his book, and a creepy sensation made him tingle as he watched a small dark figure, hunched and bent, appear in the driveway, walking toward the house.

The man looked pallid and undersized. All he lacked was a mysterious burden. Instead he was carrying a cane. But burden or no burden, Pearl didn't like him, and he didn't like her. As she ran along at one side, barking, he stopped and warned her off with his cane.

"Go away, you miserable brute!"

Tod rose and tossed his book into his chair seat.

"Pearl! Stop that! Come here!"

He walked toward the stranger, who stared at him in a fierce, bug-eyed way through thick glasses.

"I have a reservation. Name's Cartwright. My car broke down not a quarter of a mile from here. Can you tie up that animal, or something?"

"Yes, sir. I'll put her in her kennel."

"Do." The small man inspected him sharply. "Who are you?"

"Mr. Emmet's my uncle."

"Where is he?"

"He had to go over to Hynesport to take a guest to the bus. He'll be back soon." Tod collared Pearl and hauled her off in the direction of her kennel, behind the tool shed. "Come on, girl, and take it easy!"

Tod knew he had to be careful not to get any sudden yanks from the big dog that would make him stretch or twist. But he managed to coax her into her runway without doing himself any damage.

When he came back, Mr. Cartwright waggled his cane in the air.

"I don't carry this to walk with, I carry it for dogs and hoodlums, and she's lucky she didn't get a taste of it! Now, do you know where my room is?"

"No, sir, but I'm sure my uncle will be back soon, and —"

"Yes, yes, I'll wait. There should be some mail for me. Would you know where *that* is?"

"Yes, sir. I'll go get it for you."

"I'll come along and have a look at the place."

As Mr. Cartwright followed him through the house, Tod grinned to himself. They hadn't tended to that package a minute too soon. This old cane-swinger didn't look like a man who would take kindly to receiving water-soaked mail.

In the front parlor Tod opened the mail drawer and produced the package. Mr. Cartwright accepted it eagerly. Why anybody would be happy to get a copy of

Silas Marner was beyond Tod — but then, the poor man probably didn't know what he was getting. Tod would have liked to watch him open the package, but Mr. Cartwright didn't immediately do so. Instead he glanced around the front parlor.

"This looks comfortable," he said. "I'll wait here till your uncle comes back. When he does, tell him I'm here."

"Yes, sir," said Tod, getting the message. Mr. Cartwright wanted to be alone. Tod walked back through the house and out to the patio.

For a moment he stood looking down at *Silas Marner*. The book's opening page had been more intriguing than he had expected it to be, thanks to Mr. Cartwright. He picked it up, sat down, and started reading again.

He had scarcely read another page before that creepy feeling came over him for a second time.

Those pallid, undersized men were weavers, and now, in the middle of the second page, the book began to tell about how "In the middle years of this century" — meaning the nineteenth century, when the book was written — "a linen weaver, named Silas Marner, worked at his vocation in a stone cottage that stood among the nutty hedgerows near the village of Raveloe, and not far from the edge of a deserted stone pit," and went on to describe the weaver as sitting at his loom with a "bent, treadmill attitude" and having "large brown protuberant eyes" in a pale face, eyes that scared the village boys half to death.

He sounded exactly like Mr. Cartwright. And now Mr. Cartwright was sitting in the front parlor, and maybe he too was reading *Silas Marner* at this very minute. Would it occur to him that he looked like Silas?

Tod read on much more eagerly than he would have normally. Soon he discovered some traits of Silas's that were not like Mr. Cartwright's, so far as he could see. According to George Eliot, Silas only *looked* fierce, because he was nearsighted. He was really a gentle soul. Mr. Cartwright might be nearsighted, but he was no gentle soul, not with that cane.

Out in the kennel, Pearl started barking again. Tod was half afraid to look up, for fear another bent figure would appear. But no one was in sight. After a while Pearl's barking trailed off into a few final woofs. Tod had read two or three more pages when he heard a welcome sound, the brisk crunching of gravel under tires. Uncle Gary was back.

Tod was waiting beside the driveway when his uncle swung the station wagon around the circle and stopped.

"Did you get him to the bus okay?"

"Yes, we made it all right. But of all the crazy things I ever heard! On the way over M.M. told me a little more about what he's up to. Gave me some instructions, in fact, and — Well, wait till I take these groceries inside.

I just came by to drop these off and put some things in the freezer, and then I've got to run down to the village."

"I can carry —"

"Not yet, you can't. I'll take them. What's bothering Pearl?" asked Uncle Gary, as he took two bags of groceries from the back seat. Hearing her master, she had begun to whine and bark.

"I had to put her in her kennel. Mr. Cartwright didn't like her, and vice-versa."

His uncle stared at him.

"Who?"

"Mr. Cartwright. He showed up while you were gone. He's waiting in the front parlor. What's the matter?"

"Cartwright's here? Well, he's M.M.'s nephew!"

"What?"

"Yes. On the way over, M.M. told me his nephew's name was Cartwright. When I said he'd called to make a reservation, M.M. gave me his mystery chuckle and asked if any mail had come for his nephew. When I said yes, I got the chuckle again. He said he wanted me to keep tabs on everything his nephew did so as to give him a full report when he gets back tonight. And of course he repeated his remarks about the roof — 'and that's a promise!' "

"Well, it will be great if he really does pay for it!"

Uncle Gary's grin was both tart and philosophical.

"Come on, let's go see Mr. Cartwright."

They went into the kitchen to drop off the groceries and then on through the inn to the front parlor.

It was empty.

"Well, he *said* he'd wait here," said Tod. He went to the door and called, "Mr. Cartwright?" while his uncle glanced out the windows.

Tod's call drew no answer.

"Funny. I wonder where he went?"

Tod pointed to an easy chair.

"When I left, he was sitting down right over there."

A manila corner protruded from under the skirt of the chair's slipcover.

"Look! Here's the envelope that book came in." Tod picked it up. "He must have dropped it and forgotten about it when he left. He asked for his mail right away, and I gave it to him."

They went out into the front hall, and even opened the front door, which was seldom used. Most traffic in and out of the inn was through a side door and the back door, both of which opened into the dining room. The front of the house faced a high hedge across a short stretch of lawn. The hedge bordered a steep slope that dropped down to the road.

Pearl was barking again.

"Let's let Pearl out, Uncle Gary," suggested Tod. "If Mr. Cartwright's still around, she'll find him. She doesn't like him."

"Good idea."

Tod waited while his uncle walked back to the kennel. A moment later Pearl came pounding around the side of the house, skittered to a stop, and began sniffing the ground busily this way and that. Growling, she followed a trail straight to a thin place in the hedge. She stopped there, whined, and looked over her shoulder inquiringly at Uncle Gary as he returned.

"If he wanted to leave without anyone knowing, that's the way he could do it," said Tod. "If you ask me, he just came to get that book."

Then his eyes widened, and he turned to his uncle with a startled grin.

"But we've got the one he was supposed to get!"

They stared at each other. Then Uncle Gary whistled for Pearl.

"Come on, girl!" he called, and to Tod he said, "Let's go take a good look at that book!"

4

They walked around the side of the inn toward the patio where Tod had been sitting.

"M.M. said his nephew Bertie would show up, and that he would be looking for something," explained Uncle Gary. "He told me not to help him or hinder him in any way. Now, what on earth could he have Bertie looking for?"

Tod seemed to hear the scrape of the spade again.

"Something he buried?"

"Maybe. But where does that book fit in?"

"Well . . . This morning he said something about 'the Mystery Man's codes and ciphers and clues' —"

"That's right! And about how Bertie thought they were childish. Hmm!" Uncle Gary hurried forward and picked up the book from the chair seat where Tod had again left it. Resting it on his stomach, he riffled its pages thoughtfully. "Why did M.M. ask if any mail had come for his nephew?"

"Because he probably mailed him something himself."

"Exactly. And if I know that old coot's technique, this book contains a clue. Clue Number One, as he would probably put it, must be 'hidden amongst its pages.' I hate to admit it, but when I was your age I never missed one of his programs."

He handed Tod the book.

"Well, anyway, I haven't time to fiddle with this now. I have to go on down to the village and take care of a couple of errands. I just stopped by to put some stuff in the freezer, and I'd better do it. Oh, and that reminds me. Look what I found in the bookstore."

From his hip pocket Uncle Gary produced the promised fresh copy of *Silas Marner*.

"Same edition, too. Must be a popular one."

"They use it in lots of schools, I guess," said Tod. "Thanks, but I think I'll read the old copy."

His uncle ruffled his hair.

"Want to see if you can find a clue, eh? Well, good hunting. At least it will help you get going on your reading."

"I've already started it — and wait'll I tell you . . ."

In the kitchen, while Uncle Gary sorted out the groceries, Tod described how Mr. Cartwright had looked like Silas Marner himself coming up the drive, and repeated their conversation.

"That stuff about his car breaking down sounds a little thin, now that we know he took off again as soon as he had the book," observed Uncle Gary. "If he had driven up to the house, he couldn't have left without your knowing it. So he parked his car somewhere nearby and walked in."

"Maybe he was even somewhere watching till he saw you leave with M.M. He knew M.M. was going to Boston today."

Uncle Gary nodded.

"It does look as if he wanted to make sure the old boy wasn't here when he showed up. But then, why did he leave so soon? It's crazy!"

Tod was suddenly worried.

"I hope I didn't mess things up!"

"How?"

"By giving him the wrong book, I mean. M.M. said you weren't to help him — or hinder him, either. He must have meant for Mr. Cartwright to get that book, if he mailed it to him — and if things don't go the way M.M. wants them to, then his promise about the roof —"

"Ha!" Uncle Gary's laugh was shrill and cynical. "Don't you worry about that. I wish I had a dollar for every time he's talked about some grand thing he was going to do for me. Every year he talks about something, but somehow nothing ever comes of it."

"But this time he *promised.*"

"He always does that, too. 'And that's a promise!' — if I've heard that line once I've heard it a dozen times. And not just for my benefit, either. He also likes to talk about what he's going to do for the village — someday."

Uncle Gary glanced out the window toward the back lawn, smiling reminiscently, as though he could see the old man going though his paces once again.

"Every year, sooner or later, he stands out there looking down at the village and wagging his head like a kindly old patriarch, and he says to me, 'Gary, one of these days I'm going to give that little church and that library down there something to remember me by — and that's a promise!' Why, his eyes practically fill with tears, he's so earnest about it."

Tod was disappointed for his uncle's sake, but at the same time he was almost pleased in a sour, negative way. All this fitted in so well with his estimate of M.M. as a self-centered old mountebank whom it was becoming easier and easier to dislike.

"What an old faker!" he said. But instead of showing the same contempt for M.M. that Tod was displaying, Uncle Gary smiled and shook his head.

"No, don't be too hard on him, Tod. He really means it, at the time, or at least he thinks he does. Believe me, you have no idea how sincerely most people mean most of the things they say — at the time they're saying them. And anyway, who's to know? Maybe someday he really will do something. He's not the worst old fellow who ever came down the pike."

Poor Uncle Gary! He carried his good nature and his belief in people too far sometimes. Certainly Tod thought he had in the case of M.M.

Uncle Gary closed the freezer.

"Well, I'll hit the road again. Get busy, Sherlock, and see if you can crack the old master's code."

His round face suddenly became as merry as Old King Cole's.

"Bertie Cartwright, wherever you are, I'll bet *you're* not having much luck with it!"

Tod left the fresh copy of *Silas Marner* on the kitchen table with the manila envelope and followed his uncle outside.

"Bertie," he said thoughtfully. "I knew a kid once at school named Bertie. His real name was Albert."

"Albert, eh?" Uncle Gary nodded. "A. G. Cartwright. I expect you're right."

When the station wagon had gone bustling off down the drive — even the wagon bustled when Uncle Gary was at the wheel — Tod sat down again with the water-stained copy, stared at it avidly, and tried to gather together in his mind everything he knew about codes and ciphers.

It wasn't, he soon decided, much. A couple of stories by Poe and a few mystery stories he had read involved

ciphers, but he couldn't remember much about them now.

Still, the problem was fun to puzzle over, and as he sat leafing through the book, he found himself thinking about Mr. Caxton and some of the things he kept hammering away at in class, like logic and reasoning. Tod glanced at his watch, and it gave him a strange feeling to realize that at that very moment, if he were still in school, he would be sitting in his English class listening to old Wild Bill criticize a theme, or analyze a poem, or something of the sort.

Mr. Caxton was a real old-fashioned schoolmaster:

smooth silver hair, a smooth, plump-cheeked face, a figure as substantial as Uncle Gary's but without quite as much pot. A slightly nasal voice that escaped being a drone because of his own lively interest in whatever it was he was trying to get over to them. A man to whom gentlemanliness and courtesy came as naturally as breathing, and yet he could roar when he had to; he wasn't called Wild Bill for nothing. And those amazing performances at the blackboard, writing in that small but perfectly legible hand straight as a string all the way across . . .

For an instant Tod almost found himself missing school. Well, maybe that was putting it too strongly. What he really would have liked just then was Mr. Caxton's undivided attention for a few minutes. He was one of those teachers who had a way of patiently prodding you in the direction of a solution to whatever problem it was that had come up. Logic and reasoning. Step-by-step reasoning — he could almost hear him talking about it . . .

"Now, then, we have a book," he would say, "and we suspect it contains a code, or cipher, or other clue or clues. Very well. In what ways could a book be used for this purpose? Let's think about a few. For example, ciphers often involve numbers. And a book's pages are numbered. Very convenient for anyone in need of a set of numbers."

Tod began to leaf through, taking a look at each page

number, searching for any kind of mark or scratch or anything suspicious. He even held up the book in strong sunlight and looked at a lot of the pages, in case something might show through or under or around the numbers. No such luck.

"Nothing doing, eh?" he could imagine Wild Bill continuing. "May I say, however, that the examination you made was a pretty superficial one. A mere page here and there. Later on a systematic, page-by-page examination will be in order, but for the present let us consider other possibilities a bit further. First of all, we haven't begun at the beginning. The book came in a manila envelope. What about the envelope? Wouldn't it be rather clever if the book were merely a red herring, intended to divert our attention, while all the time the envelope —?"

5

Tod hurried back to the kitchen. There he gave the envelope a thorough going-over. But nothing about the typed name and address on the envelope itself suggested anything. Mr. Caxton's schoolmasterly chuckle, dry and urbane, established itself in his memory as a worthy rival of the Mystery Man's famous sound effect, and his voice resumed in Tod's mind's ear.

"Very well, then, for the moment let us look upon the envelope as having been eliminated from our considerations. And as for the book, there are so many possible ways it could be used to conceal a clue or message that we can't help but feel discouraged, can we?"

We certainly can't, thought Tod.

"In that case, let us think for a moment about M.M. and his motives. Now, a man of his experience in codes and ciphers would have little trouble constructing one that few persons could decipher, or 'break,' as the expression goes, very quickly, if at all. Yet it seems apparent that his nephew will have only a few hours, from now until M.M.'s return at five-thirty, to work on it."

Six o'clock, sir, Tod corrected him. It takes half an hour to drive back here from the bus station in Hynesport.

"All right, then, six o'clock," agreed Mr. Caxton, and Tod could imagine how the scholarly head with its smooth silver hair would respond to this correction with a courtly nod. "Even six o'clock, however, gives Nephew Bertie precious little time to work with. Now, what real fun would M.M. get out of providing a cipher so difficult that even intelligent persons, such as you and I fancy ourselves to be, would have little or no chance of breaking? Where would such a cipher leave Bertie? Hopelessly lost, and probably crying foul. Certainly M.M. would not have made his point. No, no — wouldn't the real fun come from having his nephew miss something that was right under his nose — to use his own expression — something so obvious that anyone should be able to see it?"

That's a thought, all right, sir, agreed Tod.

"A thought indeed, Tod. But now, where does it leave us? What we need, of course, is some sort of lead. Hmm . . . Perhaps our best chance for a lead would lie in trying to recall everything M.M. said this morning. Take a piece of paper and write down everything you can remember. Write on one side of the paper only, and do not abbreviate. Leave a one-inch margin on the lefthand side. For this exercise, if you do not have a pen, you may use a pencil."

I might as well be back in class, thought Tod. I'm letting my imagination run away with me! But he looked around and found a pencil and a piece of scratch paper, and brought them outside.

Back in his chair on the patio, using the water-stained copy of the book to write on, he began to jot down some of the things M.M. had said.

1. My nephew thinks the Mystery Man's codes and ciphers and clues were childish. Well, we'll see.
2. Always looked down his nose at the Mystery Man — except for trying to get his hands on some of his money.
3. Meet me at five-thirty. Then we'll have some fun!
4. Clear field for the idiot to make a fool of himself. Let him miss something any schoolboy could figure out!

Something any schoolboy could figure out! All at once the line of reasoning Tod had imagined Wild Bill coming up with began to make a lot of sense. The fun M.M. intended to have had something to do with making a fool of his nephew by showing him up. The code or cipher, clue or message, whatever it was, must be "something any schoolboy could figure out," something M.M. would really be able to flaunt in his nephew's face as having been under his nose the whole time.

And if it all had anything to do with what M.M. buried, then what he buried must be valuable, because his nephew was always trying to get his hands on some of M.M.'s money. M.M. was just the kind of mean old devil who would enjoy showing his nephew how he had managed to overlook some valuables that had been there for the taking.

Thinking about M.M., Tod felt a strong urge to help his nephew if he could. Bertie Cartwright had certainly not been an attractive person, to say the least, but even so . . . which would be the most fun? To see M.M. cackling over a mean-spirited triumph, or to see his face if he came back and learned that his nephew had broken his code or cipher and had found whatever it was the old man had hidden? The Mystery Man outwitted! Tod's grin, as he weighed these alternatives, was full of temptations to mischief.

Once again he opened his book, but this time, with a heightened sense of excitement, he opened it to the very first page. This time he would do it Mr. Caxton's way. Systematically. Page by page.

Now he examined each page with painstaking care, searching for marks of any kind, however slight. Recalling another of his teacher's ideas, Tod also took a good look at each page on the inside edge, next to the spine of the book. Whenever his classes got a new book they had to buy for themselves, Mr. Caxton said, "Choose a page you will remember, and write your name close to the spine." That way, if someone took your book, you had a means of identifying it that could not be removed or obliterated. His system cut down drastically the number of books that were stolen, and eliminated arguments about stray copies.

And since Tod still liked to think that the page numbers might be involved in some fashion, he held up each page to the sunlight, hoping to discover some mark that way.

His eyes were young and keen, but even if they were not it would have been hard to miss the little flash of light that flicked their way on page 17.

It did not come, however, from anywhere near the page number at the top right-hand corner. Instead it came through a pinhole about a third of the way down the page.

He sat up straight. New copies of a book did not have pinholes in their pages. Now he was getting somewhere.

The pinhole was under the word "Lantern."

But what about the other side, page 18? He turned the page and took a look.

There the pinhole was under the word "calls."

To be more exact, it was directly under the letter *t* in "Lantern" and the letter *a* in "calls."

"How about *that*, Wild Bill?" he said aloud, and patted Pearl joyously when she came padding up to find out if he had been speaking to her. Wagging her tail, Pearl flopped at his feet and considered a nap.

Now, if he found more pinholes, he could be pretty sure he was on to something. What if he could figure out the cipher before his uncle even came home again! He could imagine the look on Uncle Gary's round face if —

Pearl came to her feet, her floppy ears twitching, a few seconds before the sound of a car turning into the drive brought Tod up out of his chair. By that time, however, he saw it wasn't Uncle Gary.

The car was a small blue sedan, a compact.

The driver was wasting no time. Gravel spewed off the drive into the grass at the sides as he gunned his car up the slope. He pulled around the circle, stopped, and glowered out at Tod with the air of a man who went through life in a state of teeth-grinding impatience because things seldom happened the way he wanted them to. His short brush-cut hair bristled, his eyebrows bristled, his whole personality bristled.

He was a big man with a funny little mustache that seemed ridiculous in the middle of such a large, ruddy face. His shoulders, hunched over the wheel, looked about two yards wide. Behind him, sprawled sideways in the back seat, stuffing his blubbery mouth with potato chips from a huge cellophane bag, sat a boy who seemed to bulge in all directions. He reminded Tod of the lump of suet his uncle hung in a tree for the birds during the winter.

The very way the man honked his horn, three short sharp toots, seemed a criticism of the way the world treated him. Obviously he expected lackeys to come flying out to wait on him, and was infuriated when they failed to appear. By contrast, the boy stared out unblinkingly without a trace of concern of any kind, while his hand continued to slip potato chips into his mouth with all the efficiency of a conveyor belt.

The driver waited for about two seconds, then grunted his way out of the small car, while Tod enjoyed an exaggerated mental picture of a whale struggling out of a sardine can.

"Hey! Where *is* everybody? Is this an inn, or isn't it? Where's the fellow that runs this place?"

"He's not here, sir," said Tod. "He's down in the village, but he ought to be back soon."

The stranger relieved himself of an outraged snort.

"Well, I should hope so! He's expecting me! Who are you?"

"I'm his nephew."

"Anyone else around?"

"No, sir."

The stranger acted as if this were the final straw. He rolled his eyes up briefly in utter disgust.

"You mean to say he goes wandering off without

leaving anyone on duty around here? What kind of inn is this, anyway?"

The man's scorn was unfair enough to make Tod leap to his uncle's defense.

"The season hasn't started yet. He's not expecting any guests except for one who had a reservation."

"Well?" snapped the man. "That's me! I have a reservation!"

Tod stared at him, bewildered.

"I'm sorry, I didn't know anyone had a reservation except Mr. Cartwright —"

"Well? Well? That's me!" snapped the man. "I'm A. G. Cartwright!"

6

Pearl took one good look at the stranger and did what Tod wished he could have done. She disappeared, sort of on tiptoe, around the end of the house. Tod could only stand and stare. The way his mouth fell open, he knew he must have looked like the village idiot, but there was nothing he could do about it.

"Mr. C-Cartwright?"

The big man glared down at him. To Tod's eyes he looked about the size of King Kong — and King Kong in a bad mood. Nor was his appearance improved any when he bared his yellowish, block-like teeth in a sarcastic smile.

"I'm glad to find your hearing is at least functioning. Yes, I am Mr. Cartwright, and I have a reservation, and I had hoped to be received in a reasonable manner, but I can see that's asking too much around here. What about my uncle? Did he go to Boston today?"

"Mr. Murkey? Yes, sir."

"He did go?"

"Yes, sir."

"Well! That's something, at least!"

For the first time, something suited him. Gratified, he seemed to take stock of the situation and decide to switch to another approach. Tod felt as though he could actually hear the wheels turning and changing gears in the large, thick head on the bull neck above the massive shoulders. The newcomer drew in a deep breath, took hold of himself, and smiled in a new way that was obviously intended to be ingratiating.

"Don't mind me if I seem a bit upset, young man. I have good reason to be. I've had a bad morning. First I couldn't get my car started. Now that I'm finally here, your uncle is missing. This delay is very annoying to me, because I'm expecting some important mail, and your uncle told me on the phone it was here. Now, you look like a bright boy, so maybe you can help me out. Do you know where guests' mail is kept around here?"

Tod felt as though his insides were drawing together like a pioneers' wagon train faced with an Indian attack. What on earth could he reply to *that* question? Who was this man, anyway? How could there be *another* A. G. Cartwright? There wasn't much time to think about it, because the newcomer was plainly no one who would wait around patiently while Tod weighed his answer.

"Well, I — I *think* I can — er — I just got here a couple of days ago myself, so I don't know much about things, and we haven't had many guests, except one," he babbled, stalling for time, "but I'd be glad to look around. I think the guests' mail is kept in the front parlor —"

"You *think!*"

The broad face grew ruddier than ever as the newcomer's forced friendliness gave way again to his natural irritability. His ingratiating interlude had not lasted long. Now he was back to bullying. Once again the large and somewhat bulging eyes glared at Tod.

"Where is the front parlor? I'll look myself!"

"Straight through the dining room, up the hall, and to the left, sir. In the stand-up writing desk drawer."

Anything to get rid of the man for a minute. The newcomer gave him a final disgusted glance and slammed his way inside, banging the screen door behind him, leaving Tod to wrack his brains for his next move. If he had felt up to it, and Piggy there in the car had not been staring at him, he probably would have started running for the woods. But then desperation — sometimes the true mother of invention — shot an idea into his mind which seemed so brilliant that he hesitated not an instant.

Doing his best to act casual, he strolled inside. Then in a flash he was in the kitchen, stuffing the fresh copy of *Silas Marner* into the manila envelope and resealing it with the paste his uncle had used. A sound made him hurry more than ever, the sound of a car door slamming. Piggy had stirred. Frantically Tod pressed the flap down hard and rubbed it flat. Then he nearly took off for the front parlor with the package. He caught himself just in time. Couldn't do that! The paste needed a chance to dry, or it would give the whole show away.

From the front of the house came an angry bellow.

"There's nothing in here!"

Tod started so nervously he dropped the package. The complaint was followed by the clump of heavy footsteps blundering back through the house, while outside the snapping of munched potato chips drew nearer. They were coming at him from all directions! Feeling like a rat in a trap, Tod scrambled to pick up the package, and glanced around in a panic, holding it like the hot potato it was. Where could he hide it?

The kitchen table drawer! Yanking it open, he stuffed the envelope inside, closed the drawer, and ducked back into a corner out of sight as the back screen door scraped open and Piggy shuffled into the dining room. Tod tiptoed to a door that opened into the ell of the dining room and waited there till he heard the boy's father walk past from the other direction.

"Where did that kid go, Marvin?"

"Dunno, Pop."

Tod slipped through the doorway and made a wide circle of the side wing of the dining room, to make it seem as if he had come from the front of the house. Marvin saw him first.

"There he is."

The man glanced around irritably.

"Where were *you?*"

"I was looking around," said Tod. "I'll look some more. Maybe it's upstairs in my uncle's desk. Sometimes he keeps important things there."

"Does he, indeed? Then why are you fooling around down here?" snarled the big man, his protuberant eyes nearly popping out of his head as he raged at Tod. "Get going! I want that mail, and I want it now! Every minute counts!"

"Yes, sir!"

Tod scurried away through the house like a surf crab running for cover in the shoals. Somehow he had to stall for a few minutes while that paste dried. If only Uncle Gary would come home, so they could find out who this big ape of a man really was! Tod thought about the old flintlock hanging over the mantelpiece in the front parlor, and wished the darn thing was loaded. They might need it to stand off their latest visitor. He looked perfectly capable of throttling them both, and Pearl for good measure, if he got mad enough.

To kill as much time as possible, Tod actually went all the way up to his uncle's room, and by the time he got there he knew he had been running around more than he had any business doing. He was panting, and his side hurt. Nevertheless, it was well he had made the effort, because he was being followed. A crackling sound told him a fat bloodhound was on his trail. Marvin appeared and stood splayfooted in the doorway, staring in at him with china blue eyes as expressionless as marbles. With the twisted forelock of blond hair that stood up from his forehead, he looked like a poker-faced Kewpie doll advertising Krispee-Krunchee Potato Chips. Like an advertising sign, too, Marvin went in for plenty of color. He was wearing a T-shirt with blue and yellow horizontal stripes, and watermelon pink slacks.

"Find it?"

"Not yet," said Tod, pretending to busy himself at his uncle's desk. What he had wanted to do was sit down and rest for a moment, but now he had to make a great show of hunting for the mail.

"Where is it?" asked Marvin.

"If I knew, I wouldn't be hunting for it," said Tod.

Crackle, crackle, crunch, crunch. Stolid stare.

"Dumb."

"What's dumb?"

"Ought to know where mail's kept. Hick inn, if you ask me."

"Nobody asked you."

"Still a hick inn," said Marvin without a change of expression, and returned to his potato chips.

Was that paste dry yet? Never had time passed more

slowly. And time seemed to be dragging downstairs, too. Another impatient bellow bounced off their eardrums.

"Well? How about it?"

Tod winced, but Marvin never moved a muscle. One might have thought his seismograph had not even recorded this latest rumble. But then suddenly he turned his head and replied in a high-pitched yell that showed his own lung power was in the family tradition.

"He didn't find nothing! He's dumb!"

"Now, listen, you —" began Tod.

"Well, you better find that mail, or my father will tear your head off."

To give him credit, Marvin didn't sound mean about it. He sounded as though he were simply stating a fact. Tod leaned on the desk and took a deep breath. That paste had better be dry!

"Out of the way," he growled, and headed for the door. But instead of stepping aside, Marvin turned and led the way. As Tod followed him along the hall to the stairs, Marvin began taking nourishment again, and a shower of small shards sprinkled the floor.

"Hey, you're dropping potato chips!"

"That's okay," Marvin mumbled through a mouthful, "I got plenty more."

"Well, stop making a mess!"

"Bag's busted," he explained, and left still more of a trail on the stairs. Tod gave up. More important things to think about. Slowly, babying himself, using up all the time he could, he followed the trailblazer down.

"I'm sorry, I have to go slow," he explained as he neared the dining room and the man came into sight, filling the doorway, cramming it full of shoulders and a thick waist and legs so stocky they almost pulled his trouser creases flat. "I just had an operation," Tod added, and was sure from the way he felt, watery in the knees, that he looked the part.

"An operation!" The stranger acted as though Tod had undergone it just to spite him. "I come here expecting to find a proper inn, and instead I find a shambles in charge of a juvenile invalid! It's too much! I tell you, it's too much!"

"Well, anyway, I thought of one more place to look."

"You did? Where?"

"In the kitchen."

"The kitchen? Important mail in the *kitchen?*"

The man's horse-sized teeth ground the words to shreds. He stepped back to one side, shaking his head over this latest outrageous revelation. Marvin stepped through the doorway and stopped on the other side to watch. His father gestured impatiently at Tod.

"Well, come on! Have a look!"

The two stomachs framing the opening made Tod feel as if he were about to be squeezed between a large pair of rubber rollers. But he made it without loss of life or limb and hurried on to the kitchen, conscious of being followed as far as the doorway and watched from there. He opened the kitchen table drawer, took out the manila envelope, and tried to sound suitably surprised and pleased as he read the name on it.

"Here it is! A. G. Cartwright!"

"Dumb," said Marvin, but his father wasted no time on comments. The big man was beside Tod in two strides.

"Give it to me," he barked, and all but tore it out of Tod's hands. Without another word he returned to the dining room, ripping the envelope open as he went. Tod followed in time to see him take out the book and look at it with an expression that grew more popeyed than ever.

"*Silas Marner!*" he exclaimed, and for once Tod could sympathize with him. All this fuss over *Silas Marner!* The man's eyes narrowed. "Now, what does the old fool . . . ?"

Marvin's plump hand, bristling with chips, paused halfway to his mouth.

"Silas who?"

His father ignored him. Still concentrating on the book, he tossed the envelope aside in the general direction of a table. It hit the edge and fell to the floor. He pushed his way outside to the patio. The canvas chair

uttered a creaky protest as he crushed his bulk down into it.

At once he squirmed uncomfortably, and reached under himself to investigate.

He was sitting on *the* copy of *Silas Marner*.

7

Tod would have loved to give himself a good swift kick. Once again he had left the book in the chair, putting it down automatically when he heard the car coming. He held his breath while the big man glanced at the book and then back toward the door at him. It was all Tod could do to squeak out a single word of explanation.

"Schoolwork . . ."

For an instant the baleful glance continued to take him in. Then Tod breathed again as the man grunted and tossed the book aside on the grass. He began to examine his copy. Tod turned away from the door just in time to get another bad scare. Marvin was stooping over to pick up the manila envelope.

Tod leaped forward and swooped down.

"Hey, you're getting chips all over the floor again!" he cried, and using the envelope as a dustpan swept a few onto it with his hand. He was holding it by the flap end, with the flap underneath. It felt sticky.

"Not my fault the bag busted," said Marvin. "Gimme that envelope," he added, as Tod started toward the kitchen, carrying the crumbs to a wastebasket.

"What for?" said Tod, and kept going. It was lucky Marvin's father had not bothered with the flap, but had ripped the envelope almost in two across the end. And even now, Marvin would know something was fishy if he got his hands on it. Tod ripped it the rest of the way and started to crumple up the telltale end.

"Want the stamps," said Marvin.

And of course, as luck would have it, the stamps were on the flap end he was about to crumple. He ripped off the corner and removed all the excess parts, including some of the envelope's sticky back, then stuffed the remains deep into the wastebasket and returned to Marvin.

"Here, put them in your pocket."

A stamp collector himself, Tod wondered why anyone would want them. They were the commonest sort of six-centers. As he took them, Marvin's eyes glittered with the closest thing to an expression Tod had seen in them. He pointed to one stamp.

"Didn't get canceled. I can use it again," he said. The china blue eyes were sharper than they looked, sharp enough to give Tod a turn. What if Marvin had picked up that envelope? Hey, Pop, look, this is sticky! . . .

Marvin tucked the stamps away in a pocket of his pink slacks and glanced around the room.

"Got any candy bars?"

"No."

He looked unperturbed.

"Have to get my own, then," he decided, and went outside. Tod returned to the kitchen, where he sat down on a stool to give his legs and his nerves a much needed rest, and to consider the close shaves he had undergone. Well, anyway, so far, so good. At least he had the situation under control for the time being. But the sooner his uncle returned, the better. He could think of many things he would rather do than spend much more time alone with such a large man of so uncertain a temper, not to mention a pest like Marvin.

It was hard to imagine Uncle Gary demanding identification from old Man Mountain out there, but somehow they would have to find out who was who around here. If the cane-swinger was A. G. Cartwright, then who was this man? And if this man was A. G. Cartwright, then who was the small man? For that matter, maybe *neither* of them was A. G. Cartwright!

But on the other hand . . . For the first time since the big stranger had arrived, Tod had time for speculation, and now that he could think things through in a reasonably calm manner, it occurred to him that M.M. had mentioned having two nephews. Maybe that was it! Despite their remarkable difference in size, the two men certainly could be brothers. Same protuberant eyes, same bad tempers. But then, if so, why . . . ?

A nervous snicker almost slipped away from him as a thought inspired by television flashed through his mind.

"Will the *real* A. G. Cartwright please stand up?"

But if this one wasn't the real A. G. Cartwright, then Marvin would have to know his father was pretending to be someone else. Still, why not? Most kids could play along with a stunt like that if you gave them a good reason for it.

Was that why Marvin was provided with such an unlimited supply of potato chips and candy bars?

And why wasn't he in school?

From the side kitchen window Tod could see him rooting around in the back seat of the car, half in and half out, stuffing candy bars into his pockets. Backing out of the rear door, he began peeling a chocolate bar and dropping the wrappings on the lawn. Growling to himself, Tod turned his attention to the father. He was scowlingly absorbed in his examination of the book as he turned its pages one by one. His huge hands made it look absurdly small. Watching him, Tod found the King Kong image returning to mind. Certainly the man didn't seem much more intelligent than a gorilla, and in that way he qualified as a possible nephew of M.M., according to the old man's description.

For that matter, of course, the man was wasting a lot of time, intent on the wrong copy of the book. Was his brother, or whoever the cane-swinger was, equally intent on another wrong copy somewhere not too far away?

Tod's gaze shifted, drawn irresistibly to the copy that lay on the grass. If only he could get his own hands on that one again! He longed to go out and pick it up then and there, but was afraid of drawing attention to it in any way.

Then a new danger signal suddenly flared up in his mind. He had to tip off his uncle, so that he wouldn't say the wrong thing when the newcomer told him he was A. G. Cartwright!

"You're who? Why, he's already been here!" he could imagine his uncle saying — and that might be bad, very bad, no matter *who* Man Mountain really was.

A moment ago Tod had been aching to have his uncle show up. Now he was in a sweat for fear he might.

Bracing himself for an ordeal, Tod went to the door. As he stepped outside, Marvin gave him his usual unblinking stare, but his father did not even bother to glance up. Encouraged, Tod decided he had nerve enough to kill two birds with one stone while he was at it. On the way past he would stoop and pick up *Silas Marner*, casually.

Shoving the last half of his chocolate bar into his mouth, Marvin chose that moment to have a look at the book himself. Picking it up, he stared at the cover.

"Dumb," he said.

Pinwheels of frustration spun before Tod's eyes. As he walked past the boy he wanted to snatch the book out of those grubby, chocolate-smeared hands, and was almost tempted to do so, but then the whirr of tires out on the road made him quiver. Uncle Gary!

No, he was wrong. The car kept going. But the scare was enough to make him keep going, too. He dreaded the sound of the station wagon's tires on the drive ahead of him, and yet it might look suspicious if he suddenly took off on a run. Not that he felt like running, anyway.

"Walk!" he told himself rather unnecessarily, and plodded on. Down the slope of the drive he went, and around the curve to the two low stone pillars that marked the entrance, with the sign saying "The Old Manse" swinging above one of them. With every step he expected to hear a loud voice behind him suddenly yell, "Here! Where do you think you're going?" He knew he would jump out of his skin and look hopelessly guilty if that happened. He sneaked a glance over his shoulder, afraid that at the very least Marvin would have decided to tag along after him again. But Marvin was still where he had left him, watching but not moving, and his father was still intent on his book.

At last Tod was out of sight, and through the entrance. Just in time, too. He had hardly made it to the road when he saw the station wagon coming up the hill from the village. He crossed the road and waved his arms wildly.

The car stopped beside him. Uncle Gary goggled out at him in astonishment, round eyes behind round glasses.

"Tod, what are you doing out here?"

It would have been hard not to be dramatic at such a moment. Tod's gesture, as he threw his arms wide, would have done justice to M.M. at his hammiest.

"We've got another A. G. Cartwright on our hands!"

Uncle Gary's reaction was satisfactory. He took it big.

"We've *what?*"

"Another man showed up who says he's him, and right when I'd practically figured out the cipher, and he wanted his mail, so I gave him the new copy in the envelope, and now he's sitting up there reading it!"

The words came out in a rush that was too much for his audience.

"Wait a minute, Tod! One thing at a time!"

Tod jumped into the car.

"Quick, get going, before that fat little creep comes down here and sees us!"

"What fat little creep?"

"His kid. He brought a kid along, and boy, is he a pain!"

Uncle Gary drove around the next bend in the road and stopped again, out of sight of the inn.

"Now, then!"

Tod started over, filling in the details this time. When he had finished, his uncle stared at him for a moment. Then he sat back and laughed until the tears were streaming down his moon-shaped face and he had to take off his glasses and clean the steam off them.

"Tod, you're some operator!" he declared, as he worked away with his handkerchief on his face and his glasses, restoring order. "I only wish I could have been watching while you were doing all that jumping around!"

"I'm pooped!"

"I'll bet you are. If we ever get through this day, it's

early to bed for you, my boy! Hmm! Now, who the devil is *this* fellow? Well, I'll tell you one way we can find out. If he's the man who phoned me, I think I'll recognize his voice."

"Well, if you *don't* recognize it, then call the police, because this guy's big!"

"How big?"

Tod held his hands far apart.

"Shoulders that wide."

Uncle Gary took stock of the measurements, and nodded.

"I'll call the police. Never let it be said your Uncle Gary wants to be a hero."

Tod grinned.

"Good. I like my uncles in one piece."

Uncle Gary turned the car around and started back.

"I guess it would look funny if we drove up together, so I'd better get out," said Tod. Then his face fell. "But if you go on ahead, I won't see what happens when you get there!"

What Tod liked about Uncle Gary was that he understood things like that.

"All right, then," he said, "you go on back first, and I'll wait here for a couple of minutes."

Tod sprang out of the station wagon at the foot of the drive.

"But walk!"

When Tod reached the inn, Man Mountain was still engrossed in his copy of *Silas Marner*. Tod felt sure the book had not enjoyed such popularity since George Eliot wrote it a hundred years ago.

It had not, however, made the grade with Marvin. His copy had been tossed aside again on the grass, and he was busy with his potato chips, no doubt to take the chocolate taste out of his mouth. The bag was nearly empty. This time Tod picked up the book on his way past. Marvin took note, staring silently, but the man in the chair never so much as glanced up, not even when Tod almost dropped the book as his thumb skidded in a smear of chocolate on the cover.

Once inside the house, Tod stepped into the kitchen and wiped off the book with a paper towel while he stood at the window watching for his uncle. By now Marvin had polished off the last of his potato chips. Wadding up the bag, he tossed it under a tree on his way to the car. While Tod was wondering what Marvin was after now, the station wagon rattled up the drive. Man Mountain's head came up. He watched the car approach, and stood up when it stopped. Uncle Gary hopped out in his usual energetic way.

"How do you do?" he said, every round inch the genial innkeeper. "I'm Gary Emmet."

This got him a surly nod.

"About time! I'm A. G. Cartwright, and I thought you were expecting me!"

"I was," said Uncle Gary, unruffled. "I'm sorry, but I had to do some errands. Did you get your mail?"

"Yes, your nephew finally managed to locate it. Do you usually keep guests' mail in the kitchen?"

"Depends on how many guests I have. Would you care for some lunch?"

"I certainly would! Make it for two, by the way — my son is with me. My mother-in-law picked this week to start ailing again, and my wife had to go out there, so I had to keep him home from school and bring him with me. Nobody to leave him with."

"I see. Lunch will be ready in half an hour. Your room is on this floor in the front, if you'd care to —"

"Later, later. Look here, my Uncle Marvin went to Boston today, didn't he?"

"Yes, I took him to the bus this morning."

"When's he coming back?"

"He'll be on the five-thirty bus."

"Five-thirty!" Man Mountain glanced apprehensively at his watch, and abruptly sat down again with his book. "Call me when lunch is ready."

Glancing around, Uncle Gary nodded pleasantly to Marvin, who had just backed out of the car clutching a fresh bag of potato chips as huge as the first one. He gave Uncle Gary one of his unblinking stares, and started tearing open the bag.

When his uncle came inside, Tod was waiting in the kitchen, eager to hear the verdict. Uncle Gary jerked a thumb over his shoulder in the general direction of the patio and delivered his opinion in a low voice.

"A real charmer."

"Which one?"

"Well, both of them. But there's no question about one thing. That's the man who made the reservation."

Then Uncle Gary added a thoughtful comment.

"And yet, even so, what does that prove?"

"But wait a minute," said Tod eagerly. "Did I hear him say something about 'Uncle Marvin'?"

"Why, yes. That's M.M.'s first name."

Tod had never stopped to wonder what M.M. stood for. He would not have been surprised to learn that the initials did not stand for anything. But now he was excited.

"Well, that kid's name is Marvin!"

"Aha! Named after the uncle with the money, eh? That figures," said Uncle Gary. "On the other hand, if this man is only pretending to be A. G. Cartwright, then calling the kid Marvin would be a nice touch. Hmm!"

8

Uncle Gary put some lamb chops in a large skillet, thought out loud about the size of their visitor, and added a couple more. While he worked at the stove, Tod washed lettuce and quartered tomatoes. He liked salads, and knew how to get things ready for them. His uncle had made him his salad chef.

"Well, now, we've got three possibilities to work with," mused Uncle Gary, still keeping his voice down, even though the subject of their conversation was too far away to overhear it. "Either this A.G. is real, or the first A.G. is real, or they're both fakes and the real A.G. hasn't even turned up yet. All we really know as yet is that this man made a reservation *in the name of* A. G. Cartwright. But at least there's one thing we're sure of — neither man has the book he thinks he has. And nobody's going to get the right one till we *do* know who's who. Even then . . ."

He began to look troubled.

"Even then," he repeated, "how in the world am I going to explain what happened, as far as the book is concerned, without getting us into hot water? All this flimflamming we've done with those books — can you imagine how that's going to sound to our pleasant-tempered friend out there, if we ever have to tell him?"

Tod winced at the thought, and recalled Mr. Caxton unlimbering one of his favorite quotations from the works of Sir Walter Scott:

> *Oh, what a tangled web we weave,*
> *When first we practice to deceive!*

Sir Walter had said a mouthful that time. Looking back over the past few hours, Tod felt he needed a lot more practice.

"Well, we'll cross that bridge when we come to it," Uncle Gary decided. "And that reminds me — what about this cipher you figured out?"

"Well, I haven't exactly figured it out, but I've got a start."

Tod went to the window and checked on their visitors. Then he pulled the book out of his hip pocket.

"I found a pinhole on page seventeen. Or it could be eighteen, for that matter. If it's seventeen it's under *t* in 'Lantern.' If it's eighteen, it's under *a* in 'calls.' I was just going to look for more pinholes when *they* showed up."

No one as naturally curious as Uncle Gary could have remained indifferent to news of this sort. He stopped to examine the pinhole, held the book up to the light, and came to a prompt decision.

"I'll finish up here. You go to your room and look for more pinholes. If we're going to hand this book over to one of these characters, it would be nice to know first what it is we're handing over."

Tod needed no further urging. A minute later he was in his room, sitting at a little writing desk by the windows, ready to tackle the puzzle.

Turning to page 17, he started through the rest of the book, holding it up to the light of his window, page by page.

A mere dozen pages farther on he scored again. There, on page 29, under the *n* in "happen," he found another tiny pinhole.

"Bingo!"

He felt a new rush of excitement. One pinhole might have been an accidental flaw in the paper. Two were certainly not.

He checked the other side of the leaf, page 30, and found that there the pinhole was not under a word. Did that mean that 'happen' was the word, or *n* the letter, that counted?

For the moment he did not stop to speculate. The urge to continue the hunt set him turning pages again. But now the trail faded out. Twenty, thirty, forty, fifty pages went by with not a sign of another pinhole. Furthermore, he found himself holding the book closer and closer to the window, straining his eyes, and after a while he stopped to realize that the fine sunny weather they had enjoyed that morning was gone. The sky had grown cloudy again, the sunlight had faded away.

Going through the rest of the pages was a struggle, and yielded him nothing. He stayed with it doggedly, all the way to page 185, and even went through the five-page Afterword section in which a critic talked about the book. When he had examined the final page, a dissatisfied feeling gnawed at him. Were there really no more pinholes, or had he missed some because of the bad light? Had he done, as Mr. Caxton would undoubtedly have put it, a truly thorough job?

The thought had scarcely entered his mind before he could almost hear his teacher's voice saying, with that tone of patient weariness that had a way of goading you on, "How many times have I said, begin at the beginning? You found your first pinhole on page seventeen. Before that, you were not yet looking for nor expecting pinholes. How can you be sure, then, that there were none prior to page seventeen? Doesn't it occur to you that —"

Tod turned to the fading light of his window and began at the beginning. And on page 7 he found another pinhole. It was under the *h* in the word "hope."

Hope! An appropriate word. But then, of course,

there was page 8 to think about as well. On page 8 it was under the *t* in the word "North'ard."

Between pages 8 and 17 he made no further discoveries, but now that he had spotted one more pinhole he began to feel more confidence in his search. Perhaps now he had found all he was supposed to find. At any rate, the obvious thing to do next was to see if he could put the words or letters together in any way that made sense.

"Yes, I know. Write them down!" he said, grinning wryly as he anticipated what would have been Mr. Caxton's next command, had he really been present.

Tod took a pad and pencil and made himself a chart of his findings:

page 7	*h*ope	page 8	Nor*t*h'ard
page 17	Lan*t*ern	page 18	c*a*lls
page 29	happe*n*	page 30	

The question of page 30 still bothered him. He decided to take another look. This time, instead of being so intent on the pinhole itself, he took a good look at the words on each side of it, words that had not registered on him the first time.

This time they made him sit up and take notice. The pinhole was under the space between two words, and the two words were "uprooted tree."

Uprooted tree! Uprooted tree suggested earth, and earth suggested digging. The scrape of the spade seemed to reverberate loud and clear. "Uprooted tree" could really mean something! Triumphantly he wrote the words down, and then lifted his head as a now familiar bellow reached his ears from downstairs.

"What was that?" the stranger was asking. "What did he say?"

Something had roused Man Mountain again, and done a thorough job of it. Startled, Tod jumped up and hurried down to find out what was going on.

Excited talk was coming from the kitchen. Tod found his uncle in the act of turning off a radio newscast, while their guest stood leaning on a counter top, staring across at him with wild, bulging eyes.

"What did he say?"

"He said that M. M. Murkey, the Mystery Man of the once-famous radio program, collapsed in the bus terminal building in Boston this morning and was rushed to a hospital," said Uncle Gary, obviously repeating a news item word for word. "He said there is no report yet on his condition."

The big man's reception of this news was not pretty. For an instant he looked stunned. But then a slow, vindictive grin bared his large, square teeth.

"Well!"

That was all he said, but the gloating way he rolled the word off his tongue was enough to sicken anyone. Here was a man, whoever he was, who hated M.M. and wished him the worst.

But then he caught himself, and stared around him fiercely.

"Where's the phone?"

An extension handset stood on a small table in a corner of the kitchen. Before Uncle Gary could do more than point to it, the man had charged across the kitchen like a wild bull and snatched the receiver from its cradle.

Several calls later — to a radio station, a newspaper, and to the wrong hospital before he finally located the right one — he was at last talking to a doctor, and several things quickly became apparent.

"Hello, Dr. Weiss? They got hold of you, did they? Good! This is Bertie Cartwright!" he said, and it was plain from what followed that the doctor knew his voice. Who wouldn't have known that voice, once his ears had been blasted by it? So this was really Bertie. This was the real A. G. Cartwright, after all.

Some further thoughts whirled through Tod's mind, but he had no chance to concentrate on them and sort them out, because in the meantime Bertie was getting information about his uncle. After he had given the doctor the telephone number of the inn and asked him — or rather, ordered him — to keep him posted as to his uncle's condition, he hung up and pulled out his handkerchief. Slowly, enjoying himself, he wiped away the beads of sweat that had started out of his flat forehead while he shouted at various people on the telephone.

"How is he?" asked Uncle Gary.

Bertie rolled his bulging eyes toward his host.

·"He's had a stroke. He's in a coma. Can't speak, can't move. Must have been a dandy."

Whatever else he might be, Bertie was no hypocrite. He made not the slightest pretense of being sorry to hear the news. When he began to look concerned, it was for quite a different reason. His sigh was genuine· and heartfelt as he added, "He'll come out of it, though. You mark my words, he'll come out of it. He'll live forever."

Standing to one side, missing nothing, Tod knew he was seeing something unusual. This was the kind of person some grown-ups turned out to be. This was what greed and resentment and envy could do to people like Bertie, who had probably lived all of his ineffectual, untalented life in the shadow of an enormously successful uncle. But usually, when people felt the way Bertie did, they made some effort to hide their true feelings behind a shoddy veil of trumped-up emotion and conventional expressions of sorrow — "Oh, what dreadful news! Poor Uncle Marvin!" Not so Bertie. He was a brute, but in this respect, at least, he was an honest brute.

Marvin had followed his father inside and missed nothing. If the news had any effect on him, however, it was not noticeable. Certainly it did not affect his appetite. He continued to nibble without a pause. It was apparent he was used to hearing harsh words about his great-uncle and was not troubled by them.

"Maybe he'll die," he said, but as usual his father ignored his comments.

"Aren't you going to the hospital?" asked Uncle Gary.

Bertie looked at him again, thoughtfully. Then slowly he smiled, and shook his head.

"No, not yet. Why should I? I can't accomplish anything, sitting around up there in some uncomfortable waiting room. And on the other hand, here . . ."

His smile broadened and relaxed until it would almost have been a pleasant thing to see, for someone who could not hear what he was saying.

"Now I have plenty of time for *this* little battle of wits," he said, "and that's one thing the old devil didn't plan on!"

His smile burbled into a chuckle, unconsciously or not, almost a parody of his uncle's famous trademark. Turning, he glanced toward the dining room and rubbed his hands together like a man who had suddenly discovered he had a good sharp appetite. Over his shoulder he said,

"How about some food?"

9

Tod and his uncle exchanged a glance that was not so much horrified as flabbergasted. Then Uncle Gary followed Bertie into the dining room and indicated where they were to sit.

Before sitting down, however, Bertie turned to peer outside.

"Clouding up. We'd better close the car windows."

They both went out, Marvin being concerned about his back seat snack bar, and Uncle Gary bustled back to the kitchen. As he began ladling homemade clam chowder into bowls for the first course, he looked like a man trying to cope with more different emotions than he could handle, like a man who scarcely knew whether to laugh or cry. For a starter, he laughed sharply.

"Tod, I've known plenty of people who hated their rich uncles, but this ape man of ours is the first one who didn't cry crocodile tears when the chips were down. It's almost refreshing."

Tod was pleased with the way these remarks went along with what he had been thinking, but before he could say so his uncle had gone on to something else. His round face clouded with concern, and his concern was as genuine as Bertie's lack of it.

"Poor old M.M. No wonder he looked off his feed this morning. If only I could have talked him out of going! But when he has something planned, there's no stopping him. . . ."

Next he swung around from the stove, alarmed as he thought of their own predicament.

"Good Lord, now we are in a mess! I wasn't too worried about this book situation as long as I thought M.M. would be back in a few hours to straighten things out, but now it's a different kettle of fish. Now I'm darned if I know what to do!"

He fretted for a moment, and came to a decision.

"Well, one thing is sure, I'm not going to say anything about the book. We'll just sit tight until we know more about M.M.'s condition."

"I found two more pinholes," said Tod. "I was making a list of the words when I heard him yelling down here."

"Good. When we get a chance . . ." his uncle began, but dropped the subject as he heard car doors slamming and saw that their guests were about to return to the house.

"Set us up at the kitchen table, Tod. I don't think I feel up to eating in the same room with those two," he said, and carried two bowls of chowder into the dining room.

A bag and a half of potato chips and a few candy bars seemed to have given Marvin a good appetite. He crammed down an enormous meal, as did his father. When they were served, Tod and his uncle sat down to their own lunch. Uncle Gary's cooking was excellent, as always, but Tod hardly noticed what he was eating. His mind seethed with unanswered questions, questions that would have to wait till they were alone.

In spite of the amount the Cartwrights ate, it did not take them long to shovel in their lunch. Obviously Bertie was eager to get back to his book. When he had finished eating, he picked up his copy of *Silas Marner* and asked, "Now, where's my room?"

Marvin had already left the table to pay their car another visit. He came back carrying a stack of comic books and, if Tod was any judge of pocket bulges, a fresh supply of candy bars. On the way through the dining room he retrieved the potato chip bag he had put aside long enough to eat lunch. Uncle Gary led them to a front bedroom. Bertie looked around, grunted approval, and sat down to take off his shoes.

"I'll be here if the hospital calls," he said. "Shut the door, and don't let anyone bother me."

In the meantime, Tod cleared the dining room table. He was almost surprised to find some bones left on the plates. He had half expected to see that their guests had eaten bones and all.

Uncle Gary returned and poured himself a fresh cup of coffee with an air of immense relief.

"I never shut a door with more pleasure," he declared, and sat down with Tod, who was having a piece of chocolate cake for dessert.

"How is it?" asked his uncle hungrily. He was trying to diet.

"Delicious. And keep your hands off it," Tod added. He had been delegated by Uncle Gary himself to make him toe the mark, and he took his assignment seriously.

The sufferer sighed.

"Listen, I'm so nervous I need something to quiet my nerves. But . . . well, all right, I'll pass it up," he decided, as Tod poised a fork over his wrist. "Now, let's think about this mess," he suggested, his hand fumbling in the direction of a cigarette box.

"Hey, you're supposed to be giving up smoking, too," Tod reminded him. With that, his uncle threw up his hands.

"How can I give up everything when stuff like this is going on? You want to make a complete wreck out of me?"

"Mom *said* you'd never stick to it," Tod needled, and got the desired result.

"Oh, is that so? Well, I'll show her!"

With exaggerated firmness his uncle put the lid back on the box and took a harried sip of coffee.

"Don't get over-coffeed, either," warned Tod, straight-faced.

"Oh, quiet! . . . Well, now. I suppose what I ought to do is simply explain what happened and give Bertie the book."

"What do you mean, simply?"

"I know. And as I said, I don't look forward to explaining our part in all this to a man with his nasty temper. *We* know we weren't trying to pull anything underhanded, but would he believe that?"

"No."

"Besides, I don't like to do anything while M.M. is laid up. That changes the whole picture too much. We don't know what nutty thing it is that's going on between him and Bertie, but you can depend on it, something of value is involved, or Bertie wouldn't be so worked up about it. So I think I'll just sit tight and hope Bertie gives up after a while and goes away. Surely, once he gets discouraged, he'll decide he ought to be up at the hospital acting like a devoted nephew who has rushed to his stricken uncle's bedside. And then —"

A low rumble of thunder made him pause. Outside it

had grown very dark. As they glanced up, a sharp gust of wind rattled tree branches against a window. Uncle Gary took glum note of it all.

"Oh, Lord! More rain coming. I suppose just because the roof is leaking we'll hit a new record this month for total inches — or feet — of rain. Your windows closed upstairs?"

"Yes, but I'm going up anyway. I want to show you my list of the words I found in the book."

Before Tod had reached the door, though, two other sounds made him stop, look, and listen.

A car had turned into the drive.

Pearl was barking again, furiously.

A small sedan much like the one that was already in the circle, only gray instead of blue, drove up behind it. A small, hunched man got out, carrying a cane. Still barking, Pearl sidled toward him as he went out of their sight around the back of the car.

"Uncle Gary, that's him! That's the other man, the first one!"

A sudden yelp broke off Pearl's barking. They saw her beat a fast retreat, limping. Uncle Gary flared.

"Why, that —! He hit her!"

From the front of the house, heavy footsteps hurried their way. Bertie appeared in the far door of the dining room just as the other man appeared outside the screen door. The big man glared across the room at the small man. Two sets of bulging eyes warred with each other, the big man's full of astonishment and irritation, the small man's smug and yet wary.

"Phinny!" cried Bertie. "I *thought* that was your car! What are *you* doing here?"

By now Tod was wishing he were someplace far, far away, even back in the hospital along with M.M. Here was the last person in the world he wanted to see again.

Uncle Gary stepped forward. His blood was up.

"Did you hit my dog?"

He spoke so hotly that Phinny shrank back from the screen door and raised his cane.

"Yes, I did, because it was attacking me!"

"Pearl never attacked anyone in her life!"

Bertie made a bull-in-a-china-shop rush across the dining room, bumping a table or two along the way.

"Oh, shut up about the dog!" he snapped. "I asked you, Phinny, just what are you —"

"Simmer down, brother, simmer down," said Phinny, still keeping the screen door between them. "I know what you're up to with Uncle Marvin, that crazy bet he made with you . . ."

"What of it?"

"I think he's lost his mind, but if there's something to be had out of it, I want my share."

Bertie snorted, grandly contemptuous.

"*Your* share? You can go to the devil for your share!"

Phinny's lips twitched smugly.

"I thought that would be your attitude. That's why I picked up your mail."

Bertie looked understandably baffled.

"You what?"

"I picked up your mail. The mail he had waiting for you here. A book, it was, and it's in a safe place, until we come to a little agreement."

10

For a moment, as Bertie stared in astonishment, there was silence, broken only by the crunch of a potato chip. Marvin had appeared. Just by way of ricocheting an insult, Bertie turned and bounced a remark off him.

"I always thought your uncle was a nitwit, Marvin, and now I'm sure." Then back to Phinny. "Don't try to bluff me! You didn't pick up any of *my* mail, because it was right here when I came!"

Phinny gave him sneer for sneer. Stepping back a pace, he waggled his cane in Tod's direction. It's brass-tipped end scraped the screen.

"Boy! Wasn't I here earlier today? Didn't you give me a package addressed to A. G. Cartwright?"

Under the combined attention of two pairs of fierce bulging eyes, Tod felt as if he were shrinking down to a pygmy. He gulped and made the only possible reply.

"Yes. I thought you were —"

"Of course you did. I said I was Cartwright, and this boy believed me. He gave me the package, and I've got the book. So who do you think *you're* bluffing, Bertie?"

Phinny stood outside swinging his cane back and forth and looking pleased with himself. Pleasure yielded to confusion, however, as he watched his brother's reaction. Slowly Bertie turned his gaze Tod's way again.

"Then how come I got a package, too? With a book in it?"

Phinny's cane stopped swinging.

"You did what?" he squawked.

"Come in here, Phinny!"

Shock made Phinny forget his fears. He hurried inside.

"What was the book, Phinny?"

"*Silas Marner.*"

"So's mine. What the devil's going on here?"

Marvin offered a suggestion. He pointed to Tod.

"Ask him."

"I will!" Grinding his teeth together, Bertie turned his furious gaze once more on Tod. Then he stepped toward him and made a grab for his shoulder, no doubt intending to shake the truth out of him. But he had telegraphed his move to another furious man who needed only that to make him erupt into action.

Uncle Gary tore the cane out of Phinny's hand.

Whack! It came down across the thick, grasping fingers and Bertie roared with pain.

"Ow!"

Jerking his hand back, he danced up and down and tried to put all four fingers into his mouth at once.

"Keep your hands off that boy!" yelled Uncle Gary, then turned on Phinny. "And as for you —!"

He broke the cane in two across his knee.

Phinny stared unbelievingly. When he turned to Bertie, his voice was a whimper.

"He broke my cane! My good cane!"

"Yes, I broke your cane, and if you ever hit my dog again I'll break the next one over your head!" said Uncle Gary in a tone that sent Phinny backing into a corner. With half a cane poised in each hand, Uncle Gary gestured sharply. His face was red all the way to the top of his bald head. He was breathing like a man who had run a mile — on a warpath — and when he spoke, his voice was hoarse with rage. "Now you sit down and listen to me!"

A crackly thud had mingled with the other sounds of that busy moment. Marvin had dropped his bag, and his china blue eyes were protruding like a true Cartwright's. For once his mouth was hanging open without anything going into it. It was his father's mouth that was full now, full of fingers. They looked like a large enough mouthful to choke a horse, or even Bertie. He took them out long enough to sputter a threat.

"I'll fix you for this! You wait and see!"

"I'll wait!" Uncle Gary assured him. "Sit down!"

Phinny had long since melted into a chair. Now Bertie took note of the clublike way their host was holding the broken cane, and decided perhaps he had better sit down, too.

It was one of the proudest moments of Tod's life. Uncle Gary might not possess the build commonly associated with heroes, who are customarily pictured as having flat stomachs and lots of hair, but as far as Tod was concerned, his uncle would do. All at once, abruptly, Tod sat down in a chair himself, because his legs had begun to shake.

Uncle Gary glowered at the pieces of cane he was holding, and put down the handle half.

"Now, then. The last thing I asked for was to have a pair like you come crawling around my place. I don't know what this is all about, and if I had thought M.M. was getting me involved in any such mess as this I'd have asked him to leave and take his shenanigans somewhere else. But now we're into it, so now I'm going to tell you exactly what happened today."

By now Uncle Gary had regained control of himself. He proceeded to tell them exactly how the package got wet, and how he and Tod changed the books. When he reached the part about Phinny turning up pretending to be Bertie and claiming his mail, Bertie's ill temper flared again. He gave Phinny a most unbrotherly look.

"You little weasel! You wouldn't have gotten away with it if I hadn't been delayed. Of all the times for my car not to start! I had to call the garage, and it took an hour before I . . ."

His voice trailed off. His eyes bulged alarmingly. His teeth began to grind.

"Phinny! Did you t-tinker with my —"

"I don't know what you're talking about!" cried Phinny in a completely guilty voice, and leaped for his life.

"Hit him, Pop," said Marvin, but before Bertie could collar his brother, Uncle Gary had stepped between them brandishing his half cane like a policeman's nightstick.

"Hold it! You can settle that later!"

When the two men had sat down again, Bertie still seething, and Phinny still wary on the edge of his chair, Uncle Gary went on with the story. He told them how Tod had happened to have a third copy to use when Bertie himself turned up.

"You can't blame Tod for playing it safe," he told Bertie. "How was he to know you were the real A. G. Cartwright, any more than your brother — or whether either of you was the real one?"

Bertie massaged his bruised fingers with his other

hand. His ruddy cheeks filled, and he puffed out a long breath. Suspicion was dying hard, but even a man as thick-skinned and thick-skulled as Bertie could hardly fail to recognize the ring of truth in Uncle Gary's words.

"Well, I suppose . . . Nobody could think up an explanation as crazy as this one. And I do know that this boy did have another copy of the book. It was in the chair when I first sat down out there."

Then his bulging eyes glinted.

"Where is it?"

Uncle Gary glanced at Tod.

"It's up in my room, Uncle Gary."

"Go get it." He glanced back at Bertie. "Then you can see for yourself it's water-stained." He opened the door. "And I'll go put Pearl in her kennel before it rains."

Bertie's naturally suspicious nature reasserted itself. He was not one to believe wholeheartedly in anyone for long. For all his size and general clumsiness, he moved quickly now as he sprang to his feet.

"I'll go with the boy. I want to see for myself that he doesn't have four or five *more* copies to choose from. Come on, boy!"

And out of the room he went, with Tod at his heels. A sudden alarm had shaken Tod from head to toe. The list of words! It was lying on his desk beside the book, right out in plain sight!

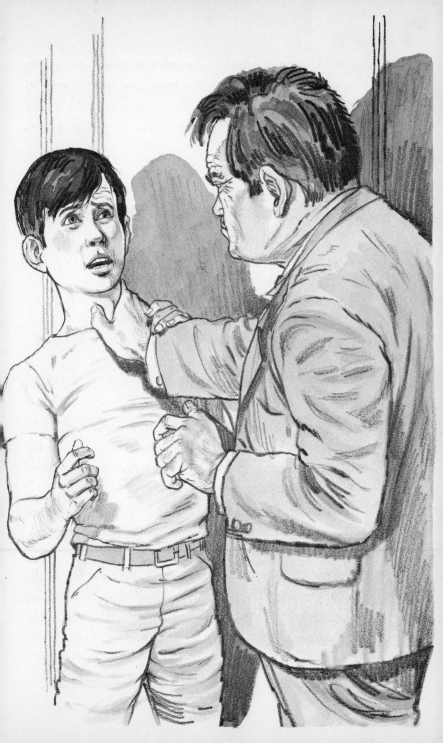

He did his best to dodge around Bertie and get in front of him, but it was like trying to get around a truck on a narrow highway. Bertie reached the stairs first, and blocked them completely as he climbed them. At the top he started along the hall, saying over his shoulder, "Which room?" but before Tod could reply he had come to the right one. Glancing in and seeing the book on the desk, he said, "Ha!" and made for it.

"That's it. You can see it got wet. It was so wet I had to stand it up in a window to dry," Tod chattered, hoping to distract the man and keep his attention pinned on the book. Maybe he wouldn't notice the list of words. Maybe he would think it was merely some kind of schoolwork Tod was doing. Maybe —

Bertie very nearly didn't notice it. He started to turn away, then glanced back. He picked up the sheet of paper, peering at it with eyes suddenly hard and searching.

"What's this?"

Tod did his best to stammer something.

"It — it's some work I was doing."

"Oh."

This time Bertie was much cleverer. This time he did not telegraph his moves. Before Tod could realize what was happening, Bertie had pushed the door shut with his foot, and the fingers of his good hand had closed around Tod's neck with the thumb placed firmly against his windpipe.

"Your uncle may be telling the truth, but you know more than he does, you little monkey. Well, he isn't here now with a cane, so if I were you I'd spit it out. What did you find in this book?"

11

This time Bertie knew what he was doing. With a thumb against his windpipe, Tod couldn't have yelled for help if he had wanted to — and he wanted to. He could sense the tremendous, frightening power of the hand that was clamped around his neck.

For a moment he reacted exactly the way Bertie wanted him to: he was scared. But he didn't quite lose his head. Bertie wasn't interested in choking him to death. Bertie just wanted to prevent him from calling for help.

Fury took over. Tod wanted to say, "You can drop dead! I won't tell you a thing!" He wanted to kick Bertie in the shins, and struggle to get away.

And then, finally — it all took only a few seconds, even though it seemed like a lifetime — finally he began to reason.

Was he guarding a national secret?

No!

Was he protecting something important to Uncle Gary?

No!

He didn't even know *what* he was protecting, but whatever it was, it didn't matter to them. But it certainly mattered to Bertie, who was glaring down at him like a madman. Maybe he *was* a madman, for that matter, thought Tod, and was suddenly much less certain that Bertie would not really choke him.

Some crazy bet an unpleasant old man had made with his still more unpleasant nephew — was *that* anything worth suffering for?

"I found some pinholes!"

Tod managed to rasp out the words in a hoarse whisper. When he did, the pressure relaxed a little — but only a little.

"You found *what?*"

"Some pinholes. Under words. Those words."

Bertie's bulging eyes went to the list in his other hand, then bored into Tod again, doubly suspicious.

"How did you know what to look for?"

"I didn't, but I knew there must be some kind of secret stuff because of the way M.M. talked. First he talked about how you always thought his Mystery Man clues were childish, and he said, 'We'll see!' And then he told Uncle Gary you would be looking for something when you came here."

"Something?"

"He didn't say what. He made a big mystery out of it."

"Ha! That sounds like him, all right," Bertie had to admit. He glanced at the list again, and suddenly his attitude changed. Tight little curls of pleasure appeared at the corners of his mouth beneath the wispy mustache. He released Tod, and even gave him a clumsy pat on the shoulder.

"Don't mind me, boy, I'm a little excited today. You'd be, too, if — Well, we'll let bygones be bygones, all right? You've probably saved me a couple of hours' work here," he declared, waving the list airily in an outrageous display of vanity.

He was so ridiculous that Tod's own attitude changed. A moment ago his only thought had been to escape from this madman. The instant he could get away he would run downstairs yelling bloody murder and tell his uncle to call the police. But now, as the sensation of immediate danger passed, the letdown left him too wobbly-legged to stir, and Bertie's clownish antics were the ruination of his anger. The whole episode was suddenly a triumph of low comedy. It was all he could do to keep his face straight.

"I only found the words," he pointed out. "I don't know what they're supposed to mean."

"Don't worry, I'll soon work out *that* part," Bertie declared with breezy confidence. He treated Tod to another of his bear-paw pats on the shoulder. "Well, we *will* let bygones be bygones, then, what do you say? Don't go down and tell tales to your uncle and get him all stirred up again. No reason we can't all work together here, instead of bickering."

Out in the hall, cellophane rattled. The door opened.

"Find it, Pop?"

"Yes. Get out of here!"

"You ought to whack him one."

"Shut up or you'll get a whack yourself. We're coming along fine, aren't we, boy?" said Bertie, and again Tod's shoulder got the bear-paw treatment. "You play along with me, and you won't regret it. If I get what I want, I'll put some nice spending money in your pocket, and that's a promise!"

With a wink he turned, scooped up the book, and clumped from the room, beaming with self-satisfaction. Tod collapsed into a chair and began to laugh, which surprised Marvin so much he lingered to watch.

"What's so funny?"

Still laughing, Tod rose, picked up a stout ruler from his desk, and gave Marvin a look that made him drop his precious bag and leave hastily, yelling, "Pop!" Tod tossed the ruler back on the desk and the bag in the wastebasket and followed quickly, but he was not really chasing Marvin. He merely did not want to miss anything downstairs.

Bertie's new reasonable mood was in full flower now.

He was holding up the list and saying to Uncle Gary, "Bright lad, that nephew of yours! Sharp-eyed. Saved me a lot of trouble here. Now, look, let's work together from now on. Just cooperate, and I'll make it worth your while, and that's a promise!"

Uncle Gary laughed.

"Now you sound like your uncle!"

"Yes, but *I* mean it!"

"Maybe so. But I can't promise anything unless I know what's really going on here. What are you after, anyway?"

They were all startled as lightning flashed brightly and a boom of thunder shook the air. A few raindrops spattered on the windowpanes. Uncle Gary closed a couple of windows, muttering, "Great! More rain!"

Meanwhile, Bertie had been thinking.

"All right," he decided, "I'll tell you. I've been trying to get Uncle Marvin to help me out with a loan. Great opportunity to make a killing on an investment, if I only had some capital — but he wouldn't budge. Only one time in his life, about ten years ago, did he ever help me out, and that was once when he thought I was really on to a sure thing and he was going to get half of it. He came through with twenty-five thousand dollars, but he made me sign a note for it, and ever since then he's held that over my head."

"The scheme didn't come off, then?"

"No, things went wrong — rotten luck — no use

going into it now," said Bertie, brushing over that part of the story in a surly tone of voice. "But anyway, this time he wouldn't budge. So last week I got mad and passed a remark about some of the nonsense he used to get away with on his radio show, and that made *him* mad.

" 'Listen,' he said, 'you couldn't find a fortune if it was right under your nose and I laid the clues in your lap! And I'll prove it. I'll give you your chance, and then we'll see!'

"Well, of course, I took him up on it. 'Put up or shut up,' I said. Then one thing led to another, and here I am," Bertie concluded. "So now you know, and you can stop worrying. It's all perfectly legitimate."

He sat down at one of the tables, spread out Tod's list, and laid the book beside it.

"The thing now is to see what I can make of this. And if you can help me in any way, you won't regret it!"

Phinny had been listening to everything from a neutral corner. Now he scuttled forward to stand behind his brother for a look over his shoulder. He had Marvin in front of him when he got there. Uncle Gary came over and posted himself behind Bertie's other shoulder. Together they all studied Tod's list.

"Hope . . . Lantern . . . happen . . . North'ard . . . calls . . . uprooted tree," read Bertie. He glanced up. "Say, turn on a light, someone. It's getting dark in here."

Phinny was nearest the light switches. As he stepped toward them, Uncle Gary said, "The right-hand one."

Peering in his nearsighted way, Phinny fumbled at the switches and flipped the left-hand one instead. Outside, the post light went on beside the opening in the stone wall where the path led out to the cottages.

Bertie looked up, eyed the light, and delighted himself with an inspiration.

"Lantern!" said Bertie. "That could be what he meant by 'Lantern'!"

Tod shot a glance at his uncle. It seemed very possible, at that. M.M. had been digging out there somewhere in that vicinity. And if "Lantern" did refer to the post lamp, then . . . The words leaped into his mind. They were so obvious that even Bertie did not take long to come up with them as he scanned the list anew.

"Lantern . . . North'ard . . . uprooted tree . . ."

His ruddy face aglow, he leaped to his feet.

"Quick, let's have a look, before it starts to rain!"

Seconds later they were all standing in a semicircle out by the post lamp.

"Which way is north?"

Uncle Gary pointed silently across the lawn, straight at a small dead tree that had gone down during a recent windstorm, one he had been meaning to clear away for a week.

"Look!" Bertie rushed forward. "He buried the stuff out here! It's got to be buried out here!"

Bertie might be stupid, but he seemed to know his uncle. And under the fallen tree, screened by the branches, he found what he was looking for. The place was well concealed. The fallen tree seemed undisturbed. The ground under it looked smooth. No one would have thought to check under the branches, if it had not been for the clue, "uprooted tree." But once Bertie moved the branches aside, signs of recent digging were unmistakable.

A lightning flash and a rumble of thunder made Tod glance around convulsively, half expecting to see M.M. again with a spade on his shoulder. But there was no M.M. this time. There was only Bertie saying in a breathless voice, "Quick! Get me something to dig with!"

Caught up in the excitement, Uncle Gary hurried back to the tool shed, where the spade was still standing against the wall. As he returned with it, rain began to fall, but that didn't stop Bertie. He seized the spade and began feverishly digging, and in his powerful hands the spade bit deeply. Ten spadefuls of dirt went flying. Then they heard the spade strike something. Metal on metal. Carefully, tensely, Bertie worked around it, brought it up.

A small black metal box.

Stooping, he lifted it tenderly, brushing dirt from its

top. At that peak instant of triumph, he could not resist a dramatic announcement.

"Fifty thousand dollars!" he said. "That's what the old fool bet me — fifty thousand dollars! And he thought I couldn't break his silly code! He thought I couldn't find it!"

He wrenched open the lid and looked in. He took out a folded sheet of paper. A smaller piece went fluttering to the ground as he unfolded the larger one, but Bertie was too upset to notice it. The sheet trembled violently in his hand. It was plain, even before he unfolded it, that he knew what the paper was.

At first he could not speak. At first he was like a man who had been hit by a bullet and had not yet felt the pain.

Then he roared.

"My note! My note for twenty-five thousand dollars!"

And slamming the box to the ground, Bertie danced up and down in a mad rage while ripping the note to shreds, as the rain began to pound down on them all.

12

For one brief moment Tod watched Bertie with stunned fascination, the way he might have watched a tornado demolish a town. Then he heard his uncle.

"Come on, Tod!"

Now he felt the rain, now the spell was broken and he could turn and make a dash for cover. When they were inside, and Uncle Gary was mopping his bald head with a kitchen towel and flicking rain from his bare arms, Tod dried himself and looked out to see what the Cartwrights were doing.

Phinny and Marvin were pretty well out of the rain under a big tree. Marvin, doubtless feeling the need for a little quick energy after so much unpleasant excitement, was unveiling a candy bar. Bertie's war dance had ended, and he was taking cover with them, but he was still waving his arms, and in spite of the storm Tod could hear snatches of what he was saying about his uncle. He was saying some harsh things. He was saying things not fit for young ears, not even Marvin's.

"I don't understand," said Tod. "Why did he get so mad?"

"Well, look," said Uncle Gary. "He owed his uncle twenty-five thousand dollars, which he never paid back, and never intended to pay back. When his uncle loaned him the money, Bertie signed a note for it. So now, instead of putting money in the box, his uncle paid off with Bertie's own note."

"Yes, but how come only half?"

His uncle shrugged.

"I don't know. That part I don't understand. If M.M. really said fifty thousand, he meant fifty thousand — I'd swear to that. But . . . well, there's something about this that still isn't clear, that's all. As far as giving Bertie back his own note goes, I can understand that all right. That would be M.M.'s idea of a big joke."

"Yes, I guess it would," said Tod, but without much conviction. Something was wrong. There wasn't time to think it all through just then, but something didn't ring true.

"Well, I thought I'd seen some cockeyed things in my day, but this beats them all. That old devil!" said Uncle Gary. "That was a pretty rough joke to pull, even on someone like Bertie."

Already the first cloudburst had slackened. The men

under the tree decided to make a break for the house. Phinny, small and stoop-shouldered, looked as woebegone as a wet crow. Bertie stamped across the lawn ahead of him, still in a towering rage. Marvin stayed put, finishing his candy bar.

"I'd better give them some towels," said Uncle Gary, and went out through the kitchen to the laundry room. By the time the men arrived, he was back.

Bertie all but took the door off its hinges coming in. When Uncle Gary held out a towel, he snatched it in a put-upon way, as if resenting having to acknowledge he had gotten a soaking on top of everything else, and began to mop his purple face and bristling hair. Behind him, Phinny took a towel, removed his glasses, and blotted them against it before starting to mop himself. Then he put them on again and stared at his brother in a puzzled way.

"Bertie, what did you mean just now when you were talking about Uncle Marvin?"

"I meant just what I said!"

"Yes, but why did you say you hoped he'd stay in the hospital till he rotted?"

Wherever he had been, — perhaps busy squirreling away his copy of *Silas Marner* in a safe place — Phinny had not listened to the news. Bertie brought him up to date without ceremony.

"He had a stroke. He's in a coma, in the hospital." He threw his brother the words the way a man attempting to concentrate on important matters might throw a dog a bone to keep him quiet, scarcely glancing his way.

Phinny gasped and goggled.

"What? When did this happen? Where is he? What —"

"Oh, shut up, Phinny, I'm trying to think!"

Stocky legs planted well apart, Bertie stood running the towel up and down his hairy arms, first one and then the other, and slowly he grew calmer. He walked over to the table where he had been sitting earlier, and stared down at the copy of *Silas Marner*. Then he turned and burst out again, but in a different way.

"Him and his tricks! I'm not going to let him get away with it. It *was* a childish cipher! Nothing to it! He was going to show me up, he said. Well, he didn't! Not with that little two-bit puzzle, he didn't!"

Tod caught his breath. The false note! That was it. M.M., the Mystery Man, prided himself on his cleverness, and yet the clues he had provided had not been very hard to find. Even without help, Bertie would surely have stumbled onto those pinholes before the afternoon was over. And once he had the list of words worked out, the right ones stood out like a sore thumb. Lantern . . . North'ard . . . uprooted tree . . .

It was all too easy, much too easy.

Similar thoughts seemed to be occurring to Bertie. His bulging eyes narrowed, he stared down again at the book.

"No, sir! I know a red herring when I see one, and this is one of his famous red herrings!" he sneered, suddenly fired with new hope, new excitement. Again it was apparent that, although intelligence might not be his strong point, Bertie did have a certain bitter understanding of his uncle and his uncle's ways.

"There's something more to it," he went on. "There's got to be. He'd never be satisfied to let me think a silly little cipher like that was the best he could do. There's something else here — 'It was right under your nose!' he'll say — and he thought I'd quit, after I dug up that box, and not look any further! Well, I'll show him. I've got plenty of time while he's lying there in the hospital, so — I'll show him!"

And with that Bertie sat down once again with *Silas Marner*. As he glanced up at the rest of them with a cunning leer, his air was that of a man getting back some of his own.

"He thought he was going to be here a few hours from now. Well, that was one place where he was wrong!"

Then he settled down to his book, leaving the rest of them to their own devices.

Peering querulously at his brother, and then at the others, Phinny began toweling himself again. Uncle Gary hesitated, but inevitably, even with men like these, he could not break the habit of being a gracious host.

"I'll get us some coffee," he said, and went to the kitchen.

And meanwhile, Tod stood transfixed, staring into space, because now suddenly there was time for a side-light to return to his mind, the vision of something he had seen at a moment when there was no chance to do anything about it. . . .

Outside the rain had slackened to a light shower and seemed about to stop. Tod nearly took a step toward the door, but changed his mind, aware of Phinny's bug-eyed stare turned his way. Besides, Marvin was still outside, and would spy on him if he saw him come outside.

Tod fidgeted for a moment and then drifted out of the room in the other direction, toward the front of the house.

He kept going through the front parlor to the entrance hall. Easing open the front door, he slipped out and went around the house on the far side. He wanted to make sure no one saw him, not even his uncle. It would not do for Uncle Gary to call out to him, wondering what he was doing out there in the wet grass under the dripping branches, getting soaked all over again, because then the others would start wondering, too.

Where was Marvin? Surely, now that the rain had all but stopped, he would walk back to the house. Or would he stop off at his snack bar? That would be bad, because from the car he could see the spot Tod was heading for. Before Tod ventured into the open, he would make sure he knew where Marvin was. He hurried on toward the low stone wall that bordered the side lawn.

When he had climbed over the wall, he was screened from the house by trees and shrubs, and was able to make his way quickly to a place from which he could see both Bertie's car and the place where Bertie had dug up the box.

When he peered out from behind some bushes to look around for Marvin, he found him.

Marvin was out where the ground was trampled, where a dozen strips of paper were lying around, the remains of the note his father had ripped to shreds. But they were not what Marvin was concerned with. He was picking up a larger piece of paper, a piece that had fluttered to the ground from his father's hand, a piece Tod had hoped no one had noticed but himself. But as he had learned earlier, the china blue eyes were sharper than they looked. While he watched, Marvin straightened up and examined his find. A twig snapped under Tod's foot, and Marvin darted a glance his way. Then the fat boy started running toward the house with a splayfooted speed Tod would have thought impossible.

"Hey, Pop! I found something!"

13

Tod scrambled through under the rain-soaked bushes and followed Marvin to the house. It was maddening to be frustrated by him, of all people, but now there was nothing for Tod to do but swallow his pride and return to the house. He did not want to miss being there when Marvin handed over his prize. What was it he had found?

When Tod came in, Bertie was staring at the slip of paper his son was holding out, and Marvin was saying, "I saw you drop it when you took out that other paper."

Bertie grabbed the slip and scowled over it, his lips moving as he read the words on it.

"Ha!"

He glanced around at them all and then read the words aloud, his tone half angry and half triumphant. By then Tod had joined the group behind him and could see the paper.

So far, no good, Bertie, my boy!
I said you couldn't find a fortune
Left under your nose
And that still goes.
So try, try again! I wish you joy!

As poetry it was terrible, but as a clue it was terrific. Bertie slapped it with the back of his hand.

"What did I tell you? I knew the old devil had something else going!"

He took on an air that hinted at intellectual brilliance. He even went so far as to turn and wink at them all as he tapped the message with a big, blunt finger.

"I'll tell you something else about this. It has the good old Mystery Man's cornball trademark written all over it. You might never notice it, but look at these capitals, the first letter of each line . . ."

He ran his finger down the line of capitals.

"S-I-L-A-S. How he loves kid stuff like that!"

Kid stuff was right. The capital letters stood out boldly, so boldly that no one could have failed to notice what they spelled. Again M.M. was making it obvious, making it hard to miss. And now there was something more, some clue that was right under Bertie's nose, something that none of them had thought of, something intended by M.M. to give him his real moment of triumph. Whatever it was, it had to be the twist created to provide the "fun" M.M. had said they would have when he returned. Tod was sure of that. But what was it?

Bertie was wondering too. His thick fingers drummed on the table.

"Well, anyway, this means the book still has the clues in it, and I'll find them if I have to —"

Bertie broke off with a violent start as the telephone rang.

"Hey! Maybe that's for me!"

Uncle Gary stepped out to the phone on the table in the kitchen.

"The Old Manse . . . Just a moment."

Bertie had followed him out. He turned and nodded. They all waited silently while Bertie grabbed the instrument.

"Yes? Yes, yes, this is Albert Cartwright . . ."

Then he exploded.

"What?"

It was enough to rattle the dishes on the shelves. With the receiver jammed against his ear, Bertie was nodding violently.

"Yes, I'll come along right away. Thank you, doctor!"

Bertie's face had been ugly enough at moments when he was angry, but now, as he returned from the phone and stood swaying on his thick legs, absorbing the doctor's message, it became repulsive with joy.

"At last!"

"Bertie!" cried Phinny. "What happened?"

Bertie stared at his brother. When he spoke, his voice was startling, because for him it was so quiet.

"He's dead. Uncle Marvin is dead. He finally did it. He finally died."

Phinny's mouth dropped open. His eyelids fluttered rapidly, as though he might faint.

"Bertie! Are you sure?"

"Absolutely. Phinny, do you realize what this means?"

Slowly Phinny's dangling jaw came up. His mouth pulled itself together again and then oozed sideways into a smile of pure greed. Tod could understand what Bertie meant. Now they would inherit M.M.'s money.

"Come on!" Bertie lunged for the door. But then he stopped. Stopped so suddenly that Phinny bumped into him. Sweeping Phinny aside, Bertie turned back to the table where he had been sitting. His glance at Tod and Uncle Gary was mocking and malicious as he picked up the book and the slip of paper. Even at such a moment he was not one to forget anything that might be of value to him.

"I'll take these along and work out the rest of it when I have time," he said. "And then I'll be back."

Now there were no more promises, no word of thanks, not so much as a simple good-bye. Out went Bertie, heading for his car. Phinny, pushed brutally aside, had half fallen against a table. He pulled himself to his feet. And after a single, bewildered, fearful, bug-eyed glance around, out went Phinny to his car.

Bertie shouted impatiently.

"Come on, Marvin!"

Marvin had stopped to give Tod a last china-blue stare that mocked his sopping wet condition.

"Beat you to it!" he crowed, and for once the plump cheeks split into a grin. The screen door slammed behind him as he ran for the car.

"Hey, Pop, can we stop at a store? I want some more potato chips!"

"Get in!"

Quickly the two cars, so nearly twins, came noisily to life as greedy feet flattened the accelerators. Tires spun on gravel, and then they were gone.

14

They stared at each other in a room that was suddenly still, and as Tod watched the changing expressions that crossed his uncle's face he thought of M.M. Maybe the old man would have been touched to know that at least one person paid him the tribute of sadness. To look at him, anyone would have thought Uncle Gary had lost a friend.

"Well, he had his faults, but I don't know what he ever did to deserve that bunch. M.M. dead! It's hard to believe. He certainly didn't look well this morning, but who would have thought . . ."

"What a family! And now I suppose they'll end up rich. I hope you at least send Bertie a bill for lunch."

"What, and throw good money after bad? Stationery is expensive."

"Well, just the same, it makes me mad —"

"Never mind, just be glad they're gone. Say, how did you get so wet again?"

"Well, I saw Bertie drop that paper, too, and went out to get it, but Marvin beat me to it."

"Oh! That's what he meant, eh? Well, anyway, I want you to get out of those clothes right away. This is a fine way to convalesce! Hop upstairs and take a hot shower and get into bed for a while. You've had enough for one day."

"I feel fine!" Tod protested, but his claim had a hollow ring to it. When he stopped to think about it, he knew he was exhausted.

"Never mind, you just get in bed and take a nap," said Uncle Gary, and teased him with a wry grin. "Where's that extra copy of *Silas Marner?* After your nap, you can get back to your summer reading."

Tod returned the grin sourly.

"Oh, sure!" Then he frowned. "But darn it, why did Bertie have to remember to take the book with him? Now we'll never know what else M.M. was up to — unless Bertie figures it out and comes back."

"And he never will," said Uncle Gary with quick confidence. "I'll put my money on M.M. for that."

As Tod headed for his room, he did not have to be told to walk. He was dead beat. He trudged slowly up the stairs, his wet sneakers crunching potato chips on every step. It was all he could do to take his shower and crawl into bed. The instant his head hit the pillow he was asleep.

When he woke up, it was nearly dark out. He was surprised to find how much better he felt. A good dinner made him feel better still. Nevertheless, when they had finished eating his uncle ordered him back to bed.

"Read for a while if you want to, but stay in bed. All we need is to have you get so much as a sniffle and your mother will skin us both alive."

On the way back to his room, he thought to take a look in the front bedroom downstairs, the one Bertie had been in after lunch. There he found what he had expected, the fresh copy of *Silas Marner* he had given him. A broad-beamed dent in an armchair cushion showed where Bertie had sat. A big cigar was ground out in an ashtray on the end table beside it, but most of the ashes were on the carpet. The rumpled condition of one of the beds showed where Marvin had rested. Where were A. G. Cartwright & Son now? At the hospital, or some undertaking parlor, wherever M.M.'s body was, Bertie probably acting very important, while Marvin sat by scattering his snack bar litter on the waiting room floor. Wherever they were, Bertie had a book with him that Tod would have given a lot to trade his copy for.

He took the book to his room, and as he settled in bed he found himself thinking about his English teacher.

"Boy," he muttered aloud, "can I ever write Wild Bill a book report on *this* one!"

An object sticking out of the wastebasket caught his eye. Marvin's second bag of potato chips. Tod got out of bed and inspected it. Hmm. Quite a few chips left in it. Shame to waste them. Might help him get through a book like *Silas Marner*. He tried one. Not bad. Nice and crispy. One thing was sure, any potato chips that belonged to Marvin were sure to be fresh. They would never be around long enough to get stale. He took the bag back to bed with him and settled down again.

Picking up his reading where he had left off, on page 33, Tod was prepared for boredom. But within half a dozen pages he began to read with growing interest.

Soon he was sitting straight up in bed, and the potato chip bag had tumbled from his side to the floor, forgotten. The story was beginning to have strange overtones.

First of all, Silas Marner had become a miser who was hoarding gold. Living alone in his cottage, year by year he piled up his gold pieces and hid them away. Meanwhile, the story turned to two brothers who lived in the village, two brothers whose father was the local squire. One of them, who was named Dunstan, was a real no-good. He was also stupid.

One foggy night Dunstan was walking home to the village, and happened to pass Silas's cottage. Thinking he might borrow a lantern from Silas, he stopped there. He discovered that the door was not locked, and that Silas was not at home.

Here was a chance to find out if Silas really had a hoard of money, as it was rumored in the village. If Silas wasn't at home on such a night, where might he be? The story continued:

Dunstan's own recent difficulty in making his way suggested to him that the weaver had perhaps gone outside his cottage to fetch in fuel, or for some such brief purpose, and had slipped into the Stone Pit. That was an interesting idea to Dunstan, carrying consequences of entire novelty. If the weaver was dead, who had a right to his money? *Who would know that anybody had come to take it away?*

He went no farther into the subtleties of evidence: the pressing question, "Where *is* the money?" now took such entire possession of him as to make him quite forget that the weaver's death was not a certainty. A dull mind, once arriving at an inference that flatters a desire, is rarely able to retain the impression that the notion from which the inference started was purely problematic. And Dunstan's mind was as dull as the mind of a possible felon usually is.

There were only three hiding places where he had ever heard of cottagers' hoards being found: the thatch, the bed, and a hole in the floor.

Marner's cottage had no thatch; and Dunstan's first act, after a train of thought made rapid by the stimulus of cupidity, was to go up to the bed; but while he did so, his eyes travelled eagerly over the floor, where the bricks, distinct in the firelight, were discernible under the sprinkling of sand. But not everywhere; for there was one spot, and one only, which was quite covered with sand, and sand showing the marks of fingers which had apparently been careful to spread it over a given space. It was near the treadles of the loom.

In an instant Dunstan darted to that spot, swept away the sand with his whip, and, inserting the thin end of the hook between the bricks, found that they were loose. In haste he lifted up two bricks, and saw what he had no doubt was the object of his search; for what could there be but money in those two leathern bags? And, from their weight, they must be filled with guineas. Dunstan felt round the hole, to be certain that it held no more; then hastily replaced the bricks, and spread the sand over them.

Tod read no further. He was out of bed now, rushing downstairs, and he was yelling,

"Uncle Gary! Uncle Gary!"

Together they examined the fireplace in M.M.'s cottage. They found the loose bricks. Under the bricks they found another black metal box. And when they opened it, they gasped. Uncle Gary's hands began to tremble so much that he set the box down on a table as carefully as if it had been a time bomb.

Hundred dollar bills in neat packets filled the box.

He didn't touch the money. He just looked at it. And when he spoke, there was fondness and an odd sort of pride in his voice.

"How do you like that? The old master knew his business. His big clue really *was* the most obvious thing in the world, and right under Bertie's nose the whole time. The *story* was the clue. M.M. knew that the one

thing a chump like Bertie would never think to do was simply to *read* the book. And not even that, really — just read the first forty pages! If he'd lived to get back here, I'll bet M.M. would have read Bertie the part you read to me, and then he'd have brought him in here and showed him what he missed. And how he would have chuckled over that part about Silas being a miser! He knew very well how often Bertie had called *him* one."

Tod nodded.

"He said it was something any schoolboy could figure out, and that's what he meant."

Uncle Gary patted him on the shoulder.

"Nice going, schoolboy! Well, come on, let's count it and see if the other twenty-five grand is all here. I never saw this much cash at one time in my whole life!"

He lifted out some of the small packets, each with a paper tape around it, and began to count the first one. He enjoyed himself thoroughly for a moment, but then his expression changed. It changed so abruptly that Tod was startled.

"What's the matter, Uncle Gary?"

"Good Lord! I just realized the fix we're in *now*. What am I going to do with this money? I can't give it back to M.M. I can't keep it, because it isn't mine. But I'd rather burn it than turn it over to those two nephews of his! Why, if I know Bertie, he'd claim there must have been fifty thousand hidden. He'd probably sue me to recover the balance!"

He was so shaken by his predicament that he put down the packet he was holding and sat down hard in a chair.

"What am I going to do?"

Tod stared at the money.

"Shall I count some of it?"

Uncle Gary waved his hand in a preoccupied way.

"No, just take it out. There were twenty-five bills in this one. I'm sure there will be the same in the others. Just count the number of packets."

Then Tod made one more discovery. As he lifted out the bottom packets, an envelope came into sight in the bottom of the box.

"Hey, look!" He held it up. "This was in the bottom."

Tod read the inscription on the envelope, and recognized the handwriting.

"M.M. wrote this! It says, 'To be read aloud by Gary Emmet in the presence of A. G. Cartwright.'"

In the silence that followed, as they exchanged a wide-eyed glance, Tod would have sworn he could hear the famous chuckle of the Mystery Man, the man who thought of everything. This would have been part of his "fun," this business of producing the box, displaying the money to poor Bertie, and then handing Uncle Gary the note to read. With an eerie feeling he watched his uncle open the envelope and take out a folded sheet of notepaper.

Uncle Gary cleared his throat.

"Well, A. G. Cartwright isn't here, and neither is M.M.," he said, "but I'll read it anyway."

Unfolding the note, he read its contents aloud.

" 'Since the childish efforts of the Mystery Man have proved to be too much for his beloved nephew Bertie,' " he began in a low voice that shook more and more as he went on, " 'the money contained herein is to be disposed of as follows: to the Bell Harbor Community Church and the Bell Harbor Public Library, $11,500 each, making a total of $23,000. To my good friend Gary Emmet, Proprietor, the Old Manse, for a new roof, $2,000. And that's a promise!' "

For a long moment Uncle Gary stared hard at the paper in his hand. Then his eyes filled with tears, and he glanced at his astonished nephew.

"You see, Tod?" he said. "He wasn't the worst old fellow who ever came down the pike, after all."